Deadly creatures

Gina Melankov

Contents

Blood prince

C hapter one

Sam smiled and placed the book he was holding on his lap and glanced over at his so called new friend, she was a young vampire girl near his age, possibly a few years older but that didn't stop him from blushing every time she said his name like any teenager who never experienced love or heartbreak.

He blinked his red eyes at the light coming through the window before turning his attention back to the conversation.

They were discussing the new book they decided to read, she pushed a strand of hair behind her ear before saying "well I thought it was quite nice except for the fact that it was awfully scary, don't you think so Sam?"

He shook his head perhaps as a failed attempt to clear his head from childish crush he had on the girl "I enjoyed it, especially the scary parts" he replied running his thumb on the cover of the book.

Before they had the chance to continue their conversation they were interrupted by shouting coming from the main hall.

As always Sam couldn't stop being his curious self and cracked the door open to listen to the now very heated argument his parents were having before a silky smooth hand touched his bare one "we really shouldn't "she said pointing to the fact that she hated eavesdropping on people ,especially the King and Queen in this situation.

This was not the first time Sam had witnessed his parents fight nor the first time they mentioned the words murder and revenge, he didn't like thinking about the rising number of guards he was forced to walk around with whenever he had the rare chance of staying out of those wooden palace doors.

He closed the door and let out a breath did not know he was holding, maybe this hopeless romance was getting to him or maybe the real reason behind him growing more worried each day was the constant subject of a broken pact.

The pact that was supposed to solve everyone's problems

Peace

Such a simple word yet such a complex concept

Perhaps they weren't meant to have it, after all his family was blamed for so many things going wrong wither it was really their fault or not, people saw them, him as a monster and Sam couldn't think of anything he could do to change that.

- Five years ago-

"Sign here "the vampire King said to both werewolf and human Kings while pointing to a doted corner on the agreement paper, finally the longest war of that era and the biggest one was over even though the witches and other creatures did not agree on signing, they only had few numbers across the continent, after all humans, vampires and werewolves all thought their own kingdom and people were the strongest, that was what originally led them into this endless war.

King James smiled even though he knew his teeth often scared humans, he couldn't change his smile nor remove his sharp teeth, he shook their hands and gave them each a copy of the truce.

"Let the festivities begin!" He shouted as trays of delicious goods poured into the big room, a fair amount of dancers gracefully made their way into the hall as music started playing softly and everyone clapped pleased by how far the three species have gotten in living in peace.

He watched from across the room a young boy who caught his attention, a human boy to be exact.

The prince reminded him of a certain someone he once knew a long time ago, a woman.

Her

Scarlet, my dear Scarlet

"Sweetheart? Did you hear what I said?" he looked up to his wife and shook the memories from his head "forgive me Wendy", but he meant forgive me Scarlet.

Chapter two

Back at the human kingdom things weren't as cheerful or pleasant

There he was laying there, his lifeless body sitting in a pool of his own blood...the human king's dead body, not only dead but murdered and without a shred of evidence on who could be behind all of this.

The body was placed there strategically and was found right after the guards switched patrols

A large muscular man in a black suit and tie walked in quietly and whispered to a man sitting across a sixteen year old human child ,making his words as low as possible afraid the teenage boy would hear him "the king is dead...murdered "and mumbled a few words before pulling away.

The man sitting across the young male was his uncle, his eyes widened and tears gathered in them but he quickly pulled himself together and walked out.

The boy was confused as he had no idea what could have upset his uncle so much, he knew his uncle as the tough man of the family so why did he look so...so afraid and shaken and sad at the same time?, his questions would be answered sooner than he thought " your uncle wishes to see you", Talia the personal boy's maid said before bowing and leaving the young prince to his thoughts

He walked up from the room witnessing a sight that made him feel goose bumps all over his skin, "Uncle Charlie? What's wrong?"

He walked to the stairs that led to the exit, Charlie holding a body rocking it with tears running down his cheeks staining his now wrinkled shirt.

the boy walked closer to find his father there dead "dad!!" he screamed kneeling before collapsing on the floor as everyone rushed to him "prince Ed !" some staff members rushed to him as one of them ran to get the doctor.

Don't forget to vote ,comment and share this story with your friends.

Chapter three

✳ becoming the king*

Ed's POV

Fear

Fear was the only thing I could feel at that moment

Running for my life through the woods barely missing a tree in the process and tripping over my own feet attempting to get a look over my shoulder at the creature hunting me

I felt as if it was a game for it ,chasing me ,materializing on one of my sides each time steering me towards a different direction ,I struggled to catch my breath as I ran as fast as my feet could carry me

Hearing some twigs snap on my right I turned to look only to find myself faced with red menacing eyes staring into my soul, I felt some kind of liquid tickling my chest looking down I was horrified to see my blood gushing out of the big gap in my chest and seeing the creature's pale hand holding my beating heart that has been detached from body.

I let out a scream as I felt the pain finally settle in my chest

"Ed? Can you hear me?" I heard a soft voice coming from somewhere above me, was I dead?i looked around trying to find the source of the echoing voice

It sounded so angelic, maybe I was dead

Suddenly my eyes shot open feeling someone desperately shaking my shoulders

"Wake up! Ed!"I watched Talia yell in my face looking worried with her eyebrows knotted together ,"stop yelling I'm up" I replied annoyed before running the back of my arm on my forehead noticing I had been sweating .

"You had another nightmare didn't you?" she asked with a frown on her beautiful face

Yes is what I wanted to say but I couldn't stand having her worry even more about me "no just dreamt I fell from a building" I lied to her face hoping she wouldn't catch on

She watched get out of bed with her hands on her hips sensing my dishonesty but not saying anything else about the subject, I looked back as I pulled out a shirt and some jeans to change into laying them on bed before heading towards the shower.

I heard her voice coming from behind the door as she spoke "your uncle is expecting you for lunch today, he's been asking about you again Ed"I rolled my eyes discarding my sweaty clothes into the hamper and getting under the shower "isn't he always?" I answered huffing in annoyance.

He couldn't let it go could he? I told him time and time again I'm not ready to be king yet and I will sure enjoy my life being free of responsibilities until I'm shoved onto a throne I never asked for ,a couple of years, that's all I had before my 21st birthday then I can kiss my freedom goodbye .

And to top that I had to choose a wife to be a queen with me, I already knew who my mind settled on when I thought about marriage and children, starting a family, but of course that was unacceptable even after being the most powerful person in the whole kingdom my uncle refused to listen to me, "she has to be of a noble family" he said.

That was only one of the reasons why I refused to have him tutor me on what to do and not do and having to put up with hours of listening to strategic military plans that I wasn't interested in.

I ran my hand through my hair in frustration and tried to shake the unpleasant thoughts from my head as I quickly finished washing up and stepped out of the shower wrapping a towel around my waist ,I wiped the foggy bathroom mirror with my palm taking a look at myself ,gripping the edges of the marble sink my knuckles turning white "tell him I won't make it Talia ,you know I never take his offer for interaction" I said bitterly and gasped stepping back as I noticed the sides of the sink crumbling into my fists as if it was made of sand.

"I understand but one of these days you'll have to accept it" her voice brought me back to reality as I dusted my hands off puzzled by the force I suddenly had, guess I didn't know how angry I was

I stepped out of the bathroom into my bedroom and watched her blush furiously realizing I was only in a towel "put some clothes on "she said shyly as she turned around "I'm not the one that stuck around while someone else showered" I teased

I was happy to have someone like her as my best friend; growing up together I was referred to as the young prince and she as girl or Talia when they actually treated her like a human being, just because she came from a servant family didn't mean she was anything less to me.

She used to get yelled at for calling me by my first name by her father as he told her it was disrespectful, but being kids we never knew what that truly meant and just went along with until I was eleven and had a fit screaming back at her father to "shut his mouth" and that she could call me whatever she liked because she was among the closest people to me and that I would have him kicked out of the palace if he ever yelled at her again.

That seemed to solve most of her issues considering he stopped pestering her and only sent her nasty looks when he thought I wasn't looking, I might be cruel but I won't lie and say I was upset to hear of his passing away due to old age and illness.

Even her mother was close to my own and as my babysitter as a child she practically raised me and told me so many memories of my own mother that I failed to meet as she had died giving birth to me, I felt a pang of pain in my chest feeling it tightness as I thought about her ,I truly believed her life would have been better off without me ending it .

Don't forget to vote and comment:)

chapter four

C hapter four

Current day

I will avenge him, I will keep his memory alive, even if it means I have to hunt down every filthy vampire on this planet

I stacked up my wooden ammunition, grabbed my guns and wooden stakes stuffing them into the black duffel bag I usually use when I go hunting, I glanced at the crossbow in my closet and decided to add it to the stack of weapons zipping the bag closed and throwing it over my shoulder I ignored a worried and angry Talia starring at me from her spot at my door.

"Don't even try T you know I'm going no matter how much you threaten me "I said while looking back at her grabbing my SUV keys and leaving my bedroom"

"That's not fair; you wouldn't want me in danger right? So why should I be okay with this?"

"because you've seen me do it multiple times already you know I'm not stopping till one of them confesses "I replied to her making my way down the stairs and ignoring the castle staff bowing to me but not missing the dirty looks some of the female workers threw her way.

I felt her gentle touch on my shoulder as she grabbed it and let her turn me back to face her as her face softened and she placed a delicate hand on my cheek making my butterflies come to life at her touch "I just wish you used a less dangerous method to find the killer Ed".

Kissing her palm and pulling her close into a warm embrace letting myself be intoxicated by her vanilla and daisies smell I kissed her forehead before letting her go and going onto my journey once more in an attempt to solve my father's murder.

*****

I stalked my pray hiding in the trees, if it were not for my unusual speed and agility I would have been spotted already, I have my weird genes to thank for that apparently I had been a bit stronger and faster than other kids my age when I was young, I always assumed they went easy on me out of respect and always let me win races and wrestling matches, now I don't know so much, it seems my strength is growing more and more every day.

I looked down at the young vampire; it's hard not to let their appearance fool you, anyone normal would think this man was human, maybe in his late twenties while in fact he must be a hundred years old, they've adapted ,learned to hide their red shiny eyes into more natural human colors to not be spotted.

I watched as he charmed a young lady with his looks and fake friendly personality, I could see his eagerly waiting for her to fall in his trap to find somewhere more private so he could suck her blood dry, they didn't care for humans ,to them they were mere juice boxes they can feed on since they were weaker .

My father never knew of the corruption in his royal council, nor did he know about the human guars that made deals with vampires in their benefit, ignoring crimes committed by them to get money or anything worthy in return.

I followed them into the empty street corner as he flirted with her leading her on, oblivious to his plan she smiled and blushed at his remarks about her beauty and grace ,I waited for the right moment just as he pretended to lean in to kiss her neck I watched his fangs extend and almost prick her fragile skin deciding it finally time to jump out of my hiding calling the bastard out.

"I wouldn't do that if I were you scum "I warned as I walked closer watching him turn to me holding the young woman hostage with his elongated fangs near her throat and now very visible red eyes and somewhat unusually long nails, he hissed at me like an animal "she is mine, I have been working on this one for days, stubborn little bitch" he spat tightening his grip on her arm as she cried softly shaking in fear finally realizing the danger she's in.

I sighed pressing my lips into a thin line "I've warned your kind about hunting in my territory, passing by peacefully is one thing, but prying on innocent humans is a crime "I watched him carefully while calculating which angle is best to take him down.

"You think your precious humans are innocent? Don't make me laugh little prince your race is as filthy as ours" I smiled watching his get distracted and pull his face away from her neck while speaking, swiftly pulling out a sharp thin stake and throwing it towards him watching it enter his mouth and poke out on the other side ,he screeched in pain and let go of the girl while I quickly went to her side and sent her home before snapping his neck and dragging him to my cellar "you and I are going to have a fun night".

vote,comment and share.

chapter five

S am's POV

He's only a weak human, how hard can it be to kill him after all?

I bet a pureblood like me can do it easily.

I opened my window looking down from the second floor and grabbed a small bottle filled with a rich red liquid and downed it quickly before tossing it into the bin in my room and jumping down using my palm and one of my knees to help steady my landing.

I looked up into the dark night scanning the area making sure to use my vampire speed to gracefully slip between the guards switching shifts for the night.

I've been attempting to get familiar with the human's smell recently; every time a new body showed up I secretly hung around taking a whiff, not creepy at all.

Making my way towards the edge of our territory and taking a big breath, one foot after the other I start making my way towards the human territory.

Once I explored enough to finally get a whiff of the familiar human's smell my body went rigid hearing footsteps close by, I crouched making sure I wasn't making any noises and tried to get a better look at the stranger.

If my dead heart could beat it would be banging out of my chest at the moment, I stalked the human keeping my distance while I follow him back to his hideout but halted when I realized I could hear a faint female voice in the distance .

I watched her place her hand on his shoulder as an affectionate gesture while she spoke "one of these days you'll get yourself hurt Ed and you won't be the only one in pain", how strange, the murderer had himself a little girlfriend, "your uncle would be devastated as well, I honestly don't think he's a better ruler than you'll be".

Ruler? Interesting, so the human troublemaker is the mortal prince, he sighed clenching his fists "I've already told you Talia I do not wish to become king "he brushed her off and walked away probably towards the castle.

Guess I know how to lure him out now; I smirked to myself and retreated to form a plan to get inside the castle, I looked around spotting some guards far in the distance flirting with some young attractive women, I hummed to myself a grin splitting onto my face.

*****

Shoving the naked body into a large trash in a random alley and fixing my outfit before making my way towards the castle and slipping in easily I start looking around the hallways for the familiar sets of smells I picked up earlier today.

Once I found what I was looking for I smiled to myself and pulled the guard gun from my waist, sneaking around the corner and clasping my hand on her mouth and starting to slowly drag her back "quiet now, you don't want your precious prince dead do you?" that seemed to do the trick as she calmed down and let me take her away.

chapter six

(i hope you liked chapter five ,so "what" is Ed? no human or vampire...
and definitely not a werewolf believe me ,what do you think he is? and
why? comment and vote and visit the website there's cool stuff there http
://jennysomething25.wix.com/jenny-something and if you really want to
feel the book go to the website to "book music " and play the song when i
tell you)

the monster that i am

Ed's P.O.V

i walked my way out of the woods going back to the castle,"you're not
human you know that right?", his words kept going through my head over
and over again, i was sinking in y thoughts ,"how can it be? my father is
human ..my mother is human...right?"

i walked in ,maids from the side of the door bowed and greeted me , i
smiled slightly at them, yes the big slayer known as "human savior" is me
,and i was nice as a puppy ...to my people at least, i know what you're
thinking ...yes they noticed the blood running down my sides and my wrist
slit opened,but hey they knew what i was doing and they also knew i didn't
want to talk about my hunt nights, "prince! are you okay?" a sharp girly

scream woke me from my day dreaming "i'm fine Talia it's just a scratch" i answered her trying to smile ignoring what just happened with that ego-ed vampire , why didn't i kill him? why did i feel like i know him somehow? , "ouch that hurt!" ,Talia was cleaning my wound and shaking ,i looked at her face ,she was so pale like she saw a ghost ,i garbed her hands , "Talia? why are you so worried it's not that bad" i said with a low tone, she couldn't look at me , i understood she was worried about me but why this much?,i put my hand under her chin making her look at me, before i knew she had colors on her face again,red my favorite color ,my uncle barged in "Ed! did anyone see s..." , i quickly let her go and walked to him "yes uncle charlie?" , he looked at me without replying for a while then he said "they told me you went hunting again", "yes as you can see "i put my wrist up for him to see , " you promised you'd tell me when you went out there ..to those...those ignorant blood suckers", "yes but you'd send guards with me, and you know i hate that"i grinned,he gave me a small smile and walked away ,"i'll be in my room" i informed everyone before going up stairs , "b-but prince y..", " drop it Talia i'll do it myself" i kept walking, yes i know...you think that was mean..but i can't let her put thoughts in her head .

i heard someone knocking i stood from my bed and unlocked the door about to open it"Talia i said drop i..." i opened the door and my uncle was in tears at my door, "w-what's wrong did something happen? is everyone okay?" questions rushed out of my mouth with no warning, he pushed me aside and walked in quietly sat on the bed" Ed..." he pointed at a spot on the bed for me to sit , i did as told, then saw him griping to a letter , "what's that?" , he didn't reply ,he just gave it to me and left in a hurry, i was still processing why he was so emotional hen i opened the letter.

Dear Ed , i know i haven't been there for you since you were a child ,please forgive me and don't hold against me ,you see..i think you're old enough to know, i wrote this letter directly to you but you're uncle knows so it's alright you can go to him when you have any type of problem ,you're the first of your kind, not a human as you thought nor a vampire or even a werewolf which is obvious because you never turned in the full moon, you're a mix of the first two, lets get to the point ,you know i love very much ,i really tried not to blame your birth for the death of your mother, but it wasn't my fault either, you see..i'm not your real father, i am sorry if you already felt that way but i's the truth, when i met your mother she was already pregnant with you and we didn't have any other kids because i can't have children, so here it is .

love ,your adoptive father.

(now play the song i told you about)

Tears rolled down my cheek, i'm not your real father,kept going in my head i burst out in tears , on my knees ,i really tried not to blame your birth for the death of your mother,it was all my fault , i killed my own mother...she loved me and trusted me, why did i even come to this world , i'm broken and no one can fix me , i don't even belong here , i'm not human ,i'm...i'm a monster.

chapter seven

(this is what you all have been waiting for)

revealing the truth

Talia's p.o.v

"drop it Talia i'll do it myself" he said to me with an annoyed face,i'm too clingy, i should obey him,he's the prince & i'm just a maid...yeah.

i walked in the kitchen wiping my tears away ,don't be an idiot ,you're a nothing to him,a loud scream snapped me out of my conversation with myself and it sounded from up stairs,i ran there ,it was from the prince's room,i knocked...nothing no answer.

should i go in? but it's rude....i don't know what to do, "p-prince?"..."may i come in ?",he didn't replying,although i could hear him breathing and crying quietly,i'm going in i don't care if he gets mad at me,he needs someone to be there for him,come on man up!! The irony I opened the door and peeked in,i couldn't believe my eyes,the prince was laying on the floor staring at the sealing and crying,just crying,then i noticed...he was still bleeding , i bet it hurts,but for some reason he didn't care, i opened the door more and slowly walked in,"p-prince?...are you alright?",he looked at me ,he didn't yell at me for coming in or answered my question...of course he's not alright what did i expect?...,i walked towards him and sat ,he just stared but at least he stopped crying,then suddenly he gripped me into a hug,a strong firm hug,Ed is hugging me...i mean his majesty...oh god he's holding me,i could feel his strong muscles around me ,should i hug him back?...i'll go for it, i slowly lifted my arms on his back and squeezed him tight, a tear fell on my neck..it was so cold,then he puled back & i let him go ,he wiped his tears and stood up" t-thank you Talia but i need some time alone now", "alright please call me out if you need anything prince " i got up," call me E...", "i didn't hear you ", "nothing...Talia nothing", "okay " i bowed and left closing the door behind me.

Ed's P.O.V

i walked in the bathroom trying to collect what was left of my manhood after weeping like a five year old girl ,what's got into me?,why did i leave my walls crash down in front of her?, it doesn't matter .

yes it does you schmuck

shut up.

you can't shut yourself up smart ass

yes i can

prove it

...whatever go away

o_O

40 minutes earlier: Sam's P.O.V

i walked out of the woods slowly making sure that no one notice , "Sam?! what the hell went thru your head ?!" my dear father was shouting at me, "i'm fine !" i replied annoyed , "you better start walking towards the castle before i drag you to it " he threaten me,"fine." i didn't bother arguing because i know he would actually do that....yeah i have a crazy dad get over it.

i walked beside my dad quietly fixing myself while grinning from people's reaction from seeing the royal family walking between them...oh boy you should have seen their faces so shocked , i looked at a little girl who was staring at me then bend towards her changing my eye color to red as she made no noise just stared "boo!", she screamed as loud as possible , "oh shush little thing i'm just messing with you " her mother rushed pushing me away and grabbed her "we don't want you here blood suckers! shoo!" , "how rude , listen i wouldn't hesitate to r-..", "shut it Sam!" , "..y-yes father" , "i apologize for my son's behavior please forgive him, he's young and foolish" my father said to the woman holding her child " , she just made an angry face and walked away" , my head got hit hard "ow, father!" , "one more word and i'll tie you to a tree and leave humans do all they please with you" , i knew he was serious so i nodded .

" what the ..." i woke up bleeding on the floor looking at a some black boots, i looked up, "you again!" i tried to stand up but everything was spinning , he grinned and then started laughing like crazy scientist.

Ed's P.O.V

i heard loud knocks on my door "come in!" , i walked out of the bathroom drying my face from water, "sir some civilians informed us that the vampire king and his son are here in the town, could they want an agreement or something? i put on my usual black clothes back on and took some guns and swords and ran to the village, i spotted them immediately, i mean who could miss two people in fancy clothes with 20 or more guards in black, i waved to my people and they quickly got everyone out of my way, then i walked behind them without making any noise , i slit all the guards's throats before they could talk, don't want to blow my cover now do i?, finally i had a one on one with the little brat , right when he was turning to face me i git the back of his neck with my sword's wooden end i was holding it from, i couldn't help but laugh, i mean seriously? you're a bloody vampire and i knocked you out with one hit ," stop! please" i searched where the voice was coming "we come in peace, please we mean no harm, my son ran to face you and i came to take him back, i apologize for making your people feel threaten ", oh well then king seems different from his son...somehow there's good in him, then the son woke up , i looked at him , his face was hilarious ,like he was drunk or something so i laughed really hard not even trying to hold it in.

.

chapter eight

(did you like chapter seven? if you did make sure i know, vote and comment and the most important go to the website http://jennysom ething25.wix.com/jenny-something if you have suggestions don't hesitate i'm open minded , and here comes the surprise in this chapter, finally right?)

come again?

Ed's p.o.v

"you do realize it doesn't matter to me, one of your kind broke the agreement and killed my father, i'm killing you anyways" i said waving my sword as i spoke, "yes but that would mean losing your real father" I froze slowly turning to face him once again

"what are you talking about?", "i know Raymond wasn't your biological dad....son"

wait what? what did he just call me?

i'm positive it was 'son'

oh you again

you mean 'me' again

this isn't the time for this ,shush

"are you listening?", "what..", "i said i'm your father and this is your little brother...well half brother ..Sam"he said pointing at then teen vampire

WHAT IN THE WORLD IS GOING ON?!!

everything was blur i felt like i was in a bubble, i couldn't hear properly i couldn't speak or move,my life is a lie? really?! i just found out that my dad isn't really my dad and now a blood sucker telling me i'm his son, it can't be, i never anted to taste blood and i ate human food.

"i know you're confused son y-..", "don't call me son , i'm not your son", "you are but alright i wont, listen to me carefully, you're mother and i were in love , i was willing to marry her but her parents didn't agree obliviously because i'm not human , but we still saw each other in secret, but then...her parents introduced her to him...Raymond, he was charming ,nice and human so she fell for him, unfortunately she was pregnant , and he knew but didn't mind, he just wanted her to be his forever but "karma" happened as you humans call it, she died giving birth to you."

Sam's P.O.V

what?! no , he's my brother?!! , anyone but him, but...that means i wont be king anytime soon...oh come on give me a brake!

the dizziness went away and i could stand again, so i did "what do you mean he's my brother?!! i can't believe this, and you didn't even tell me", "well you're not good with secrets son"

"so you KILLED HIM?!!" that annoying human shouted, "no no it wasn't me i swear on my thrown"my father said, "...why should i believe you?" ,"because i'm your dad?" , "look...this is just...too much for me right now let me process this and i'll come to you if i have questions..now leave ,you're scaring my people" , "actually they aren't 100% your people " i grinned but my father shushed me with a hit on my head, what? i'm just messing with him...ugh.

Ed's P.O.V

i feel numb,I've never felt like this before , it's just...blank, a vampire is my father...i never thought something like this could happen to me , I didn't know hybrids existed ..?

He walked home that night , wounded, not on the outside but on the inside.

Not knowing who he was anymore

He needed to find himself again,find a reason to live

To fight back and survive,thinking it through ...maybe he had one and never noticed it,but still,being a half breed wasn't going to be as easy as being a human.

(surprise! if you wanna see it go to the website http://jennysomething25 .wix.com/jenny-something then click on characters drawing and it works on phones so yay)

chapter nine

❋ i think i lo...*

uncle charlie's P.O.V

"i'm home", i heard my nephew say as he silently walked in, I've been waiting for him for almost an hour now, was he okay?, do i even need to ask ? obviously not,he's a man now ,but he was still a child in my eyes, how can a person go through so much and still find the will to be alive?, i should let him rest, but not alone ,i don't want him to do anything stupid, "Talia" i called, "yes your majesty?" she responded behind me, i smiled a little knowing she wanted to help him through as well as she could, i whispered "escort him to his room and stay with him at all times ,try not to tell him i ordered you to but say it if it's necessary ", "yes your highness".

Talia's P.O.V

i said as he ordered ,slowly following the prince without invading his personal space,he walked in such a different way now, his head and arms dropped down ,if they weren't attached they'd fell on the floor,so much pain was surrounding him ,he looked twenty years older , a different person he became.

Ed's P.O.V

i could hear her following me, i didn't want her to but she can't help it,i felt so heavy,i wanted to cry but i couldn't,i just kept moving trying to hold it together ,i opened the door to my room and walked in,she did also without saying a word, i depreciate it,that she didn't ask ,she wanted to know,but gave me the choice to tell her or not,"close the door behind you", she did as told,i sat on the bed putting my face in my hands,should i tell her?, of course i should she's my best friend,"please sit", again she did as i asked,i could feel her waiting for me to spill it out, so i did.

"i'm not human"i said while looking at him from time to time,she didn't say anything at the begging ,then she finally spoke, "what do you mean?", "well..i am human ,but only half", "and the other half?" she stared puzzled "..um..vampire", "vampire as in...drinks blood?" , "yes..i just found out..R ay isn't my biological father...James black is", she stood and walked around the room for a while then sat down next to me again,she took my hand and squeezed it, "that doesn't change anything to me" and gave me a wide smile like if i told her i wasn't vegetarian or something, so thoughtful, that's how she always have been,a tear escaped my eye,but it wasn't a sadness tear ,no, that was something else, something i haven't quit known just yet,she wiped it gently,"when you're sad , a piece of me dies ", "Talia" ," yes prince?", "first..call me Ed , and second...i think i love you",she smiled and blushed like a tomato, "i think i love you too ..Ed", i intertwined my hand with hers and put my free hand on the back of her soft neck ,feeling her silky hair with my fingers and slowly leaned forward , she came closer, i closed my eyes and gently pressed my lips against her lustful red lips ,i moved them around hers slowly making the kiss deeper,i hardly controlled myself and puled away.

(yay they finally kissed, did you like? comment and vote and don't forget to check the surprise on the website http://jennysomething25.wix.com/ jenny-something love you all xxooxx)

.chapater ten

✱ i didn't mean to hurt you*

Ed's p.o.v

i had a shower and changed my clothe ,Talia was sleeping,and no we didn't do anything ,i sat next to her,looking at the beautiful woman i hoped being mine,so peaceful and quit,she looked her best while sleeping.

i took off,to the vampire king,i had lots of questions and needed answers.

"you can't go in there" said the guards, i smiled and walked forward,one of them grabbed my shoulder ,i glared at him"touch me again and that hand wont touch anything again",he seemed confused, "he's right you know" that annoying teen vamp again"come one big bro lets go inside",i followed him but kept myself ready for anything"where's James?","in the garden","so we're going there ?, "yeah",i followed him while looking around trying to figure out exits as much as i can "relax no one's going to attack you" ,"says the guy who bit me", he rolled his eyes at me ,what did he expect ?that I'd just trust him?

"hello Edward "a gentle smile came across my eyes, "hi..","lets go to my office", "okay"i followed James with his son on my side, or should i say my 'brother'. i don't even know how i should act..

"come in please " he opened the door for me leading the way", i followed,silently ,"so what did you want to ask me?" , "uhm...wh-what do i eat? i mean I've been eating human food since i can remember...i never drank blood","oh..you can drink both", "okay..and can i run as fast as you guys?and do i have fangs?do i have any skills?", he smiled"yes, yes and yes they didn't show yet?","no ,everything's been normal","alright ,that's all you wanted to ask?", "well all i can think of for now..i should get back home now"i walked to the door and opened it, "you're welcome here anytime son", "okay...thank you"

on my way home i thought about things,maybe this isn't so bad,i have some power or as James called them 'skills', i wonder what they are,back at the castle i saw the excited Talia waiting for me,i smiled,wow i realized i haven't had a real smile in ages,i can understand that from the view,cute and adorable almost childish look on her face like a kid waiting for Santa,i'd love to see her this happy all the time,"ahh Talia easy on me", she giggled and stepped off the hug-tackle she did to me"sorry Ed ,too exited, you've been gone for long,"well the walk took all my time i actually didn't stay that long there..lets go inside" i wrapped my arm around her shoulder protectively,she snuggle against my chest, i bet she can hear how fast my heart is beating for her,good.

******

i closed the door to my room behind her,took off my shirt,it was dirty and sweaty, i guess i walked alot, though i didn't feel it,"are you okay?","hmm?..oh yes i'm fine just thinking sorry",she smiled at me then lost herself somewhere staring at me shirtless , i smiled then she touched a spot on my left side, a scar,a memory,"what's this from?", "one fight that went wrong,it was my first vampire,almost left my skin there", i desperately tried to make it a joke, but failed ,she didn't take her eye off it,"ugly isn't it?","no, don't say that...it's a proof that you're a survivor Ed,do you realize how dangerous what you do is?","don't..just don't ,don't try to protect me ,im not a child, im way too powerful then you think", i tossed on a clean shirt and turned around"i don't need this kind of talk from you, i had enough from my uncle","...you know you're mother wouldn't like it", i angrily turned to face her, "don't you dare talk about her, you don't know her, you weren't even born,how could you know a nice lady like her? you're just a maid!",she stepped back looking down, "you're right..im just a maid", she ran before i could stop her,"Talia! wait i didn't mean that!",she was already gone as i stepped out,i really didn't mean that,why do i always let anger take over....?

because anger is all you know

...

you don't know love,kindness,happiness, all you know is anger, sadness, sorrow, pain

i really don't want to talk to you.., i mean myself

but you are.

(comment and vote, visit the website mestirios6.wix.com/blood-prince)

chapter eleven

(sorry for taking so long on this chapter my wifi was down ,don't forget to vote comment and visit the web site mestirios6.wix.com/blood-prince)

****

i would never hurt you

Ed's p.o.v

Here i was ,two days after Talia dumped me,i'm tired of this mess,always something happening in my life ,cant i just be normal?,well i need to figure out how to make Talia forgive me,if that's even possible.

I set up a nice dinner in the garden, white silky cover on the table ,candles at the middle,white plates with pink tulips on them,her favorite ,i planed keeping her busy and off the garden,the staff was happy to help,i'm so nervous,is she going to like this?,maybe the surprise will get her off guard.

Oh come on!,are you going to talk about 'feelings' and rainbows and butterflies?

well if that would make her forgive me then yes.

*rolls eyes*whatever dumb ass.

after the chit chat with my smug inter voice i gave the sign for the maid who was responsible of getting Talia nice and dressed to let her in.

"hey"

"hi..um what's going on Ed?"

"just sit please"i made a hand gesture towards one of the chairs,"...alright"s he sat,i pushed her chair in as a gentleman,then sat facing her,i poured wine in both our glasses and took a deep breath,"Talia..i just need you to know..i never meant what i said,sometimes i just act like a jerk,you probably do know how my mother was considering your mom was her best friend...i'm so sorry ,and you're not just a maid", i smiled and kneeled on one leg facing her and held her hand"you'll be my wife ,if you desire that of course",i caught a sparkle in her eyes,"i..i forgive you and..yes ,i'd love to"she gave me a big smile and i did the same then quickly pulled out a small box from my pocket,and took out a ring with a tulip shaped diamond on top ,i slowly and carefully placed it on her finger"you look beautiful ms Johnson or should i say Mrs rainheart"i smiled while getting up and holding her tightly in my arms "i love you","i love you too Ed" .

***(after the wedding)

Mr and Mrs

Talia's p.o.v

i opened my eyes to see a Greek god sleeping next to me,so handsome , so vulnerable wouldn't believe that he was a killer,i gently kissed his forehead and slowly slipped out of the bed careful enough not to wake him ,then a firm grip help me by the wait"e-ed?",he laughed and pulled me back"where do you think you're going cutie?",i smiled as he placed me in his arms,where i belong"i thought you were still sleeping",he brushed my hair slowly"can a pirate sleep after finding his treasure?",i couldn't help but giggle,oh how handsome he is without all those clothes hiding his beautiful skin.

" it's not that good you know"

"hmm?what is?"

"my skin,you said it was beautiful"

"Ed...i didn't say it,i thought of it"

"you what?"

"yeah..i think you're vampire genes are starting to kick in"

"wow, reading minds?so cool"

"ugh..."

"what?"

"now you're gonna know everything i think about..."i pouted

"mhm ,like how good i look without clothes on?"he whispered in my ear,i blushed red.

chapter twelve

✳ new generation*

Talia's p.o.v

I rushed to the bathroom ,threw up everything i had this morning,Ed came after me and held my hair up,he's been so sweet and gentle ...even you know when,i washed my mouth and cleaned my face then took a shower,wrapped a towel around my body and dried my hair with another one,"you've been sick for two days now,we should call a doctor","im fine Ed ,maybe i just ate something bad","hmm...one more day then I'll get the doctor","okay fine"i got dressed ,fixed my hair and put on light make up and my lovely ring,i gazed at it,so beautiful,Ed knows me so well,"i'm glad you like it"he hugged me tightly into him,he had such a soft touch,i closed my eyes and lost myself between two worlds,"Talia?honey wake up","uhmm...my head hurts "i tried to get up but quickly lost my balance,thank god Ed was there,he picked me up bridle style and placed me on the bed carefully"what happened?","you fainted..i don't know whats wrong ,i checked your body ,you're not bleeding or hurt,just rest now ,you need to freaking regain energy"he covered me with a blanket ,i soon realized i wasn't in my dress ,i wore a comfortable night gown and my jewelries were on my night stand,i let sleep take over until i woke up to find my lovely husband at the bed just staring at me"hi", "hey"i smiled,"how are you feeling?"he held my hand tightly","better,much better",i sat up slowly"take it easy you don't need to get up if you cant","im fine"i swung my legs at the side of the bed,he held me by the waist and arm"just slowly "i nodded and gat up taking baby steps,i felt okay ,i slipped away from him"so you don't need me anymore ?"he gave me a sad face,i smiled"of course i do ,just not to help me walk"i took more steps and was finally myself again,i took a deep breath,that's better,"good"he sat on the bed carefully watching me.

blood,hungry.

"did you hear that? "he walked towards me,i nodded"no what is it?","did you think of blood?",i stared"no why would i?",he walked around the room listening ,"there's someone else in the room"he walked to the closet and with on move jerked it open,nothing,then he peeked under the bed,nothing,he opened the door,no one,"it doesn't seem that anyone is here Ed","shht"he came closer and pointed me to move aside,i did as told,he looked behind the closet,nothing again,then he turned and gazed at me,"come here for a sec hon","um..okay"i walked towards him,he held me ,closed his eyes and listened,then suddenly a smile appeared on his gorgeous face,"honey...you're pregnant."

chapter thirteen

----

ed's p.o.v

I walked in my...father's castle holding my wife by the hand "its okay dont be scared","im not,i have you to protect me"i smiled at her then walked towards the office"hey big brother!" my anoying sibling tackled me ,"oh my god sam! can you be carefull? i almost draged talia with me"i gat up cleaning my clothes"who?"he stared at me,"my wife ,come here honey"i watched my beautiful wife walk towards us,im surprised the pregnancy is barely showing, i puled her by the hand closer "sam ,this is talia my wife,talia this is my anoying brother",his mouth formed a big o as he looked at her from head to toe,"stop drooling"she said while snaping her finger in his face and smiled"hmm sharp and sassy,i like her already"he laughed slightly, "dont forget im a vampire talia"he flashed his fangs at her,she grined and held my hand"well this guy is a vamp too and look how scared i am"she said while pointing at me,"my manhood is hurt"i put on a sad face and whiped invisble tears "aww i didnt mean it like that honey"she kissed my cheek and smiled, "by the way sorry i couldnt come to the wedding i had werewolf buisness ",i grined"so where's dad samy?","uh..i dont know did you check the office?", "i was about to",wow his brother is kind of handsome ,altho he sounds competetive and big headed,"he's nice when you get used to him"i whipered in her ear,she blushed "stay out of my head you"i smiled "nope i need to know who else you think is handsome",she play-pushed me "being tough huh?","um..love birds ,dont mean to desterb you but when are you gana open the door?"my lil bro said while looking at us,"yeah ,the door,right"i opened it and peeked in,"ahh ed! come in please","um...dad remember talia ?","oh yes you're wife,i met her at the wedding,is she okay?","well ..its not that "i pushed the door opened to let him see her,"oh my...congragulations son,he gat up and puled me in a hug "thanks dad,but theres some things we need to ask you"i put my hand in my pocket, "of course please come in"he puled away and huged talia gently "nice to see you again",she gave him an honest smile"nice to see you too dad ",we steped in taking a seat facing his desk,he walked around it and sat down"so what do you want to ask me you two?"he leaned back into his chair,talia squezed my hand tighter,"well...i was woundering,is it safe?i mean a human carying a half breed?",he sat straight"yes i believe so,she just needs to rest and feed him/her alot",i jumped forward"yes!about that,what is she sopose to eat?,she's still eating human food but ...blood crossed my mind 'cuz...i heared the baby ask for it",he rised an eyebrow in question"the baby asked for it?","yeah i heared his/her thoughts", he looked at both of us"well you should try it out then",there was a few moments of silence, she's more my age ,why did she marry my grompy older brother?and she's really cute..

"i heared that!" i snapped at sam who was deeply going through inapro-preat thoughts about my wife, "sooorry"he replied innocently,"whats that about?"talia whispered in my ear,"just..my brother being himself"i gave her a small smile then turned to my dad"is the baby gonna have the same powers as me?",he smiled"of course not...everyone has their own powers son ,and i can't wait to see my grandchild's " he smiled into the air ,i gat up snapping him off his memories, " we should get going " ,he stood p aswell "yes of course" he gave me a quick hug.

after three mounths

Talia's p.o.v

Im getting bigger,talia said to her self rubing her baby bomp,she looked in the merrior and couldn't wait to go to the doctor's apointment ,today they find out the gender of the baby.

I smiled feeling my husband holding me, frankly im getting used to him coming out of nowhere and holding me i gigled, he almost gave me a heart attack last week when i was in the shower and he toched me, i screamed at the top of my lungs before he quickly shut me up with a sweet kiss, "you better get used the other stuff too Mrs rainheart"he said while smiling against my neck,"shall we ?", "absolutly my dear wife",we walked out heding to his black rang rover,what's with boys and cars anyways ?,after a few talks about names and the nursery that was still in progress we were there, i took a deep breath,"ready honey ?", i nodded and steped off the car waiting for him which never happens in the house considering he was able to use his vampie speek there, he gave his hand to me nd i took it without any hisitation,once i was laying there with jello on my tumy the stress was going higher and higher,"calm down it's not like he's gonna say the gender is cheez", i smiled, could he be serious at all ?, "congrats Mr and Mrs rainheart you're having a little girl" the doctor anounced, i smiled and quickly foccused on ed's face trying to read his reaction,he kissed me "i can't wait to meet her" he smiled from ear to ear, i was releaved because i didn't know which gender he prefered having, most man want a boy so i'm still nervous about the whole thing,"don't be,i'm the happiest man just knowing that it's our baby", i smiled.

Once home he insisted on anouncing it to his father and brother,his step mom was nowhere to be seen afer the "revelation",anyways here we were holding pink shoes while walking in the black's residence,"dad ! sam ! come here quick !",i watched my excited husband calling them ,in a blink of an eye they stood there with a questionable look on their faces,"is everything okay son ?" then ed steped towards his father and waved the pink shoes in his face,"a baby girl dad, a beautful little girl"he said as his eyes started tearing ,his dad puled him into a tight hug,"i'm so happy for you" he let go of ed"did you choose a name yet ?", ed looked back at me and gestured for me to joint hem, i did so"well we had lots of names but eventualy there were two left jason if i twas a boy and rose if a girl, so i guess we're going with rose ?" he looked down at me which was snuggling against his wram chest like love struck puppy, " yeah i guess so" i gave him a smile then suddenly noticed that sam wasn't behind james anymore, he was at my side just staring,then ed noticed"aren't you gonna congragulate us ?"while squezing me tighter to him, was it just me or they couldn't stand eachother sometimes ? ,"of course"sam put on a fake smile"congragulations"he held ed in a brotherly hug then hugged me which in my opinion took longer then it should .

A/N :we havnt talked in a while guys,enjoying the book ?, if yes let me know by voting ,commneting even messaging me or on the website which you have a memory lost if you dont have it memorised in your head by now,anyways what do you think is going on in sam's head ?maybe you want a sam's p.o.v ?, leave the answer in the comments plz i'll change the next chapter with your requests, and also there will be big surprises so remember to breath, and new characters are coming in chapter 16 or so ,love you all xxooxx.

chapter fourteen

B lood prince

you deserve to live

Six months later: Talia's p.o.v

I looked around everyone was sweating and breathing heavily as if after a fight, I saw ed looking down at something, I reached for him but my hand went right through ,"ed?what's going on?",no answer, I got closer and peeked to see what he was looking at, at the horrifying seen I screamed as loud as I could while looking at...

"wake up baby, you're having a nightmare", someone was shaking me, I slightly opened my eyes to see ed's worried face looking at me, I was out of breath"i-I saw..",he interopted"I know baby , I know"he held me tight trying to comfort me, I started feeling pain,a lot of pain so I pushed him away to see a frown froming on his face"whats wrong?", "ahhh! It hurts"I kept saying over and over while holding my belly.

Ed's p.o.v

I was horrified ,my wife is having our child, RIGHT NOW!, "breath honey" I quickly picked her up to see the wet sheets under "you're water broke" I started to move toward my father's room since he insisted on having us every weekend, "dad! DAD!" I yelled while speeding out towards the car, I put her in the back seat laying and breathing hard, I didn't waste time turning when I felt him behind me "it's time?" I simply nodded as I stepped in the driver's seat and turned my car keys roughly as it started "calm down "my father said already sitting next to me and smiling, as I drove like a maniac to the hospital I noticed the scratching marks on my arms and felt the ones on my neck, I chuckled realizing my dear Talia was in so much pain that she didn't even care if she had to chop off my head to stop the pain.

**

"push baby push" I demanded her while she griped me like a tiger, after some screams ,pushing, sweat and not feeling my hand anymore I heared a small scream and this time it wasn't talia, I turned around to see a nurse cleaning a very small baby then handing it to me"hi there little rose"I leaned on Talia to let her see our gorgeous baby girl, she smiled wide "rosy" the name barely came out of her mouth after all the fatigue holding her prisoner.

Once back home Sam was all over rose,making faces and kept going on about how cute and small she is, everyone was busy with the kid when we heared howls and barks...oh no.

After two hours of arguing with werewolves ,making sure that they know once they attack we wont spare any of their kind,it might seem selfish that I wouldn't care if I had to kill a werewolf female but couldn't live if my talia or little rosy died,that's just my human side being like this,talia was griping me while we sat there listening to bangs and loud knocks on the door "give us the baby and no one will be hurt" as if, but now you could see who was really afraid them,guess from who, yup a baby, a new born,and there was no way I was letting them toch my angel both of them,little rosy was asleep in my arms,then a loud noise made us all jump from our places,time to fight,I handed rose to talia and james ,sam and I stood forward protecting them,"that thing is a freak", thing?,freak?,I lost it I jumped on the big werewolf as he shape shifted and dug my fangs in his neck,surprisingly he didn't black out,he just smiled then jumped towards talia and rosy ,everything went in slow motion as I froze,no matter how hard I tried I couldn't get my feet to move,I was so angry at myself,"DAD!" I heared sam scream, we killed the two others and rushed at his side, my dad had protected talia and the baby,he covered them just in time as the wolf dug his teeth and claws into him,sam was sobbing while rocking him quitly,"please dad..dont go"he managed to say with a low voice as tears ran down his cheeks,his last words were "ed....*caugh caugh*..take the thrown".

It happened again

My dad died.

chapter fifteen

✳ death is my bff*

Ed's p.o.v

Sam didn't even show up at the funeral, he just stayed in his room for days,without feeding or talking to anyone ,whenever we tried to get him to do something he'd just stare at use until we leave.

Losing my biological father,that i just started to get attached to and felt a bit like family is gone.

There's no going back.

And again...guess who's fault it was?, yup mine.

Rosy's been growing fast,too fast, and now dad isn't even here to say if that's normal or not,days..weeks passed and werewolf attacks are only getting stronger and more often,we lost a lot...humans...vampire and still this war is just beginning ,although we out number them by uniting humans and vampires ,but still humans can't do much,I wished if that anger and rage that helped me through the years to kill would float to the surface ,it didn't, I just felt...numb.

"..umm you okay?",oh god yes, finally he spoke,I gave him a small smile"I'm fine little bro"and I messed up his hair,he smiled,he smiled! Omg,my joy was suddenly interrupted ,"ED!!, HELP!", talia..oh no, I went to her as fast as I could,there she was, pinned against the wall by the throat with a stinky doggy,how didn't I smell him? Or sam?,no time to think I had to act , I jumped on his back ,sinking my fangs in his neck as deep as I could,he growled and yelled releasing talia to the ground,I placed my hand on the sides of his head and jerked it hearing a loud crack ,good,I ran to her,"are you okay?", "y-yes" she barely said between coughs "where's rose?",my eyes widened"where did you leave her the last time you saw her?"I quickly blurred out,she pointed at a room,before she could talk I was in that room"rosy?,honey where are you?!"I shouted when she was nowhere to be seen,of course, talia was only a distraction,I closed my eyes and listened searching for rosy's three year old heart,"found you"I opened my eyes and rushed outside to see two wolfies holding my little girl"take you're hands off her!","or what?you'll tell your daddy?,oh wait he's dead!"they laughed,I could feel anger running through my veins,no one is dying this time,I can't live with it,I could feel sam by my side as ready as I was"let's kick some ass big bro"he said,and with that we lunched forward biting,kicking ,punching and chocking anything but rosy, a few more bites and punches later they were done,I let out a breath ,as my little princes ran to me crying,"daddy!","it's okay honey ,it's over now"I kneeled to her level and hugged her tightly,I must have been dizzy because I smelled talia and three different werewolves, alive wereworlves,what the h-..,I got punched so hard that my nose broke,I looked up holding my bloody nose to see two wolfies holding my dear talia each from one side, and the bastard that hit me grining,thiscan't be happening,NO!,NO!,I looked back and sam was pushing rosy behind him in an attack stand,I looked ahead again to see one of them holding talia's head tilted ,"I love you.."she said and closed her eyes"NOOO!!"I jumped on my feet and ran when the same guy who hit me grabbed my legs, "you're just supposed to watch blood sucker", *crack*" TALIA!!"I screamed at the top of my lungs before seeing darkness.

chapter sixteen

B lood prince

new girl

Sam's p.o.v

I never thought my life could change so much in one year...talia, I miss her,and poor ed...he already tried to take his own life twice if it wasn't for the guards who kept an eye on him for me.

Yeah he's taking my place, I kind of hated him at first but now...I'm glad im not an only child,child,little rosy...she'll grow up without a mother,at least I didn't let her see that horrifying scene last mounth,talking about the kid...I should call someone to help out ,I mean she needs a feminine presence in her life,I picked up my phone and dialed a number,"yes...dena?,how are you?...yeah you heard huh?, I'm fine don't worry but I need a favor..yeah can you come over?...great see you then".

I keep knocking and he keeps ignoring me damn it...,"ed! Come on open up you need to meet someone.

Ed's p.o.v

Why wouldn't he just let me die?, he knows I can't live without her , I wrote a poem for talia I smiled wide just when I remember it , "I'll read it for you baby "

I'm trying to protect you from me

The monster that should never be

It's too hard to stay away can't you see?

To me no girl reaches you to the knee

Disappearing is the only way out

I'll always love you there's no doubt

Seeing you happy is what it's all about

I can't take it anymore I want to shout

I chuckled at myself, talking to a dead wife,I swear I'm sane,then I heard loud knocks and my name "talia?", I opened the door to see tall girl with pale but glowing skin, short hair,long legs, grey eyes, I've never seen that color before, "yeah yeah she's pretty we get it" I blinked and look at sam who woke me from an awkward staring,if you were in my shoes you'd understand, through my life I never saw many girl, and the once I saw looked normal, not ugly just normal,but her...she looked like an angle, angel...Talia , I made a long face and stepped , back at the end of the room staring at nothing, "ed snap out of it..Please focus"I glared at sam"...okay","this is dena,she's a good friend of the family, we can trust her", she reached out her hand, I hesitated first but eventually took it , "and she's here because...", I raised an eyebrow in question, " Dena Gabriel Jones at your service your majesty"and she bowed, polite..but I still don't trust her, how can i?,"I called her ed, she can help with rosy".

Dena's p.o.v

Wow I never thought he was this attractive and by the way he looked at me I can tell he feels the same towards me, I shook his hand ,introduced myself and bowed, I hope I can help his kid, my father told me what happened, poor family was tore apart because of a helpless child, I also did some research, turns out this man had lost his biological mother due to his birth and his adoptive father was murdered awhile ago , he's been through a lot, and now he lost his father and his wife, sam said they were married for a bit over a year, that's so sad, he barely started his life and it crumbled underneath his feet, yeah life isn't fair I guess.

"may I meet the child your majesty?"I said as politely as I could, "yes and call me ed.."he walked a few steps then paused , he must have remembered something, "are you okay?" I heard sam say while squeezing his arm slightly, "I'm fine".

Ed's p.o.v

'call me ed' is what I said to talia when I first started having feeling for her...angles aren't suppose to die, and she was my angel, I felt the hesitation in dena, she doesn't know if she should say something or not , add that to her early thoughts, of course I heard that 'I never thought he was this attractive' , yup she's definitely after my father's thrown, I need to keep an eye on her, maybe sam trusts her but I don't.

"daddy!" , "heeeey princes" I hugged my daughter as I walked in her room, you'd think a little girl's room should be pink and covered with flowers and rainbows, think again because this one is half a vampire and we're well known for liking the two colors , red and black, exactly what the room if filled with, plus she's been through hell which explains the lack of colors in her life.

"who's the pretty lady daddy?" she asked while peeking from behind me , "this is dena honey, she'll stay with you all the time " , " will she play with me too?" I smiled , what an angel"yes, and when you need anything ask her, I'll try to visit you as much as I can though" she frowned when she remembered I was still leading the vamp army through the war.

"hi there little one "dena said while kneeling at rose's level , rosy grimaced and smelled her, dena seems confused and a bit uncomfterble , "sorry she always does that with new people, memorizing their sent", "oh, that's alright" she smiled at me,"should I trust her dad " rose looked at me , I don't like her,yeah that was rose mind speaking with me, we recently found out that she can do that but i have a feeling that it's not her only skill, "trust is earned "I responded while smiling at dena back , oh yeah she got the message.

chapter seventeen

* she's good with kids*

Ed's p.o.v

I carefully watched Dena through these last four days she's been taking care of my dear rose, and of course I did the same with her thoughts, I needed to make sure my little girl was safe.

Today I decided to stick around and spend some time with rosy , and having an eye on Dena was just a perk , so I walked towards her room when I was about to knock I heard rosy say "Dena...why did my mommy leave me and daddy?" , I stopped and looked down , I knew there would come a day when questions that but I hoped she's ask me , not Dena, "well...everyone leaves at one point little one, and we all have a right time for that , but when we leave it doesn't mean we don't love our family and friends anymore...it just means that god needs us somewhere else and he knows that our loved ones are strong enough without us...and you're a strong girl aren't you?" , I opened the door slightly to see rosy's sad face paint a smile on itself , "uh-huh , I'm strong !" then she roared , I smiled at the fact that she was able to make my little girl smile while I couldn't many times , I took a deep breath and knocked " who is it ?" I heard rosy say , "draculaaaa!" I sang loud and barged in running after her , she was screaming , running and laughing all at the same time , it took Dena three seconds and some blinks to understand it was a game , at that moment she exploded in laughter so hard that tears would form if she wasn't a vampire and was trying to control it so hard , vampire don't actually cry but they can , I cornered rose and started to tickle her and got a quick reaction as she started laughing like a maniac until she begged me to stop, so I did, "you're daughter is quit something Mr. rainheart " , I turned towards her and smiled " Ed ..Dena, call me Ed" , she bowed "as you wish " she paused for a while "it's time for your bath princess" and she walked towards her , rosy pouted " but..but-but I don't want to.." then started to wiggle around not letting Dena catch her "please rose don't make this hard on me" and she tried to grab her gently but rosy snatched her arm away and crossed her arms , 'rose, go take your bath right now ' I told her in my head and she frowned "but daaad..." , now!, after glaring at me with an angry look she finally did as told , Dena was confused as hell as she looked from me to rose as if it was a ping pong match and not quit understanding what just happened , after rosy went to the bathroom she Dena finally spoke" your majes-...uhm..Ed , what just happened?", I smiled, "that was our mind speak, you see..i read minds and it turns out rosy can hear mine too and we worked with that making it a privet talk just between the two of us" I explained , "oh..that's..unusual " , " yes, she's a very gifted child" , I smiled but couldn't help but notice how Dena's face changed to different colors in a small amount of time, " is something wrong?" , " I ...I um", omg omg he heard me the first day we met , I called the future king'attractive' oh god what if he thinks I'm just a slut or after him because of who he is i...,I grabbed he shoulders "it's okay , it's no big deal , I mean you're attractive as well..." I choked what did i just say!?

You called her 'attractive' if I'm correct

Oh my god! now she'll think I like her or something..

You don't?

Uhm..i ..umm shut up me!!

I snapped out of my slightly insane mental state to see the beautiful Dena blushing red as blood and staring down not bulled enough to look me in the eye , I quickly noticed my hand was still on her shoulder so I pulled it back " I'm..I'm sorry I shouldn't have said something like that" I scratch the back of my neck nervously as she looked up gaining some confidence "it's-it's okay ...Ed , I said the same or rather thought of the same thing..."she looked away refusing to meet my gaze , I slowly leaned closed pulling her attention back to me, just inches from each other then i.."Dena! , didn't you say I need to take a bath?!" screamed rosy behind the bathroom door , talk about right timing.

***

I was in my office when the bell rang, vampire , I could feel it and hear his thoughts , I missed Dena so much, I hope everyone has been nice to her she was so nervous on the way here ,great she has a boyfriend and I almost kissed her , I heard the door being opened "Jake!" I heard Dena yell with excitement, ugh awesome, then I saw her hugging him tightly and he spin her around , I coughed gaining their attention as he stopped spinning her and they both focused their eyes on me ,"greetings your majesty , please forgive us for the noise we're making in your home" and he bowed , I walked towards them" it's perfectly fine..." , "Jake ,Jake Keith Jones " he held his hard towards me , I shook it , Dena couldn't stop smiling and looking at him , " this is my brother " she said with a smile , my mouth formed a perfect "o" , I looked like a teen age when I was jealous, jealous? What?! , ugh I'm getting too close to this girl ,I thought to myself.

A/N: all of you Talia fans don't give up on the book stay ton ;)

chapter eighteen

✱ I miss you...*

Ed's p.o.v

It's been over three months now since I lost my love , rosy's all grown up looking like a twelve year old , she's more mature now , she stopped asking about her mother last month , and Dena has been a real help , she even got in a fight to protect rose during a werewolf attack and I own her for that , she took a lot of hits and managed to keep rose unharmed there wasn't even a scratch on the little one when Sam and I finally came to the rescue , rosy's been practicing on fights , I wanted her too, at least if she does get kidnapped she can fight back a little until we arrive , although she's been a bit sad that her powers didn't show yet , I'm sure they will soon, but the good news is that she trusts Dena now and has a really nice girl bond with her , I know Dena can't take away the pain or ever replace her mother but it's better than nothing , the coronation has been pushed back for obvious reasons which are:

1)   the crazy war going on

2)   I don't have a queen by my side for me to become king

And with that said let's get back to the present time.

"you wouldn't dare!" I snapped at Dena , " I would" she grinned like a devil and instantly threw and egg at my face, I could have dodged it but I wanted to do this, "you better run young lady!"I said while popping in her face getting the fear reaction I wanted from her, she was about to run but I grabbed her wrist and with one rough move I pulled her crashing against my hard chest ," ow, ed!" she pouted, "oh shut up it didn't hurt that much" I replied , she blushed red when she realized her hands were on my chest and mine were on her waist ,our gazes locked in a long stare , I hesitated first but I pulled her closer , she was surprised but replied by slowly placing her arms around my neck , I smiled then started leaning closer as slow as I could to give her time to back away if she wanted , and she didn't , I kissed her gently , moving my lips against hers and tilting my head to deepen the kiss, she moaned slight , we could have done that the entire day but sadly we heard a loud cough which made us both jump away from each other ,Jake ,decided to ruin the moment on his sister and I , it was a bit awkward and embarrassing but hey this is my house and I didn't force her to it, "sorry to interrupt but…but the blackwoods are waiting for you in the office prince" he said while scratching the back of his neck avoiding my stare , "right" I replied a bit annoyed then looked at Dena for a brief moment " stay with rosy..I'll see you later " and I gave her a small smile , she simply nodded.

Me and jake walked in the hallway silently until he decided to say" so you really like my sister don't you?" , "I do "I Stoll a glance from his face to see his lips twitching into a wide smile "just be good to her " , "I will" , we finally reached the office , I fixed my tie and before opening the door and stepping in , everyone greeted me respectfully and bowed , the blackwoods informed me about some information about a savage new born(new turned vampire) who went through towns and sucked the blood out of humans but left them alive, it surprised me , usually new born vampires can't control their blood thirst and kill humans by accident while feeding on them , they also said it was a woman , I wonder where the hell whoever turned her was for allowing her to be so irresponsible .

Vampire law, rule 173: a vampire shall keep his new born under constant control and a well behavior , any feeding from an unwilling creature is considered a crime which will allow the council to decide the punishment of both new born and his/her master.

" and your saying her master was nowhere to be found?" I questioned one of the royal investigators , he avoided eye contact as respect and answered " yes your majesty " , I was irritated because I couldn't go on the field and do it myself "send some guards to find the new born and bring her by force if necessary" I signed some papers as everyone nodded and left .

I frowned at the sight of a report which was sitting between papers I was signing I can't believe it wasn't found , I thought to myself , I snapped my head towards the door , "come in" , she cracked it open slight and poked her head in "I need you to see something dad " she glared at me , "alright I'm coming princess" , "daaad , I'm not a baby anymore" I chuckled , "but you are a real princes remember?" , she rolled her eye and gestured me with her hand to follow her , and I did.

"what's going on?" I walked in rosy's room to find : Dena , Sam and Jake already there , sam smiled widely at me "just sit and watch big bro" , alright this is weird ,I thought as I sat , rose faced me and put a pencil on the floor then preceded to close her eyes , she breathed calmly and started raising her arms slowly , I was too shocked to speak at first ,the pencil was floating the same way her arms moved , and with a sharp quick move she gestured to the left with her hands and the pen was stuck to the wall with a loud noise ,"ohmygod!" I yelled.

chapter nineteen

✳ moving on*

Dena's p.o.v

I wonder what's the surprise that Sam was talking about is , I put on my best dress like Ed told me to , oh Ed , just the thought of him makes me want to melt , the curves around his muscles , his messy black hair , amazing black eyes that seem to swallow me whenever I look at them , I can't stop thinking about the kiss , even though it was for just a few seconds , it felt like eternity as I fit perfectly in his arms ,I suddenly felt nervous , every time he touches me I feel weak and vulnerable and at the same time I feel confidante and strong.

Once finished with my makeup and jewelry I stepped out of my room walking towards Ed's , I put my knuckles up about to knock when he opened the door , " I hate it when you predict my every move.." I crossed my arms against my chest , " you look beautiful Gabriel " I blushed a reddish pink hearing him call me by my middle name then I made the mistake of looking at him , he wore a classic black pants not too tight not too lose, a sky blue tight shirt with three opened bottoms allowing me a view of his chest muscles , his hair was a messy " i-kinda-care-how-it-looks" look that made me giggle , then I found him smirking which made me realize I was biting my lip, I blushed again looking at the ground, he held my waist with one hand and the other one intertwined with my hand ,with a graceful movement he pulled me inside and closed the door with his foot refusing to let me slip away.

We looked up from the balcony into the clear deep blue skies, a bright star caught my eye and I stared forgetting that he was still standing next to me , I let out a breath feeling the night cool breeze brush some hair away from my eyes , he gently slid his arms under mine onto my wait and held me tight , he rested his head on my shoulder then kissed it gently ,"you're perfect" , I melted into his deep soft voice and closed my eyes "I'm so far from perfect Ed..." , "you are to me...but I wanted to ask you" he paused and togged some hair behind my ear ," yeah?" , "are we dating?" ,I sensed his muscles tense and I knew he was nervous, I turned around and looked into his amazing black eyes then pouted like a child ,"you never asked me to" and I crossed my arms on my chest , he smiled wide and looked up , "forgive me Gabriel...I couldn't get myself to do it knowing that she died because of me" he refused to look me in the eye and proceeded to glare at the stars , I frowned at the view of my beloved so sad ,"it's okay you're forgiven" , he looked at me and smiled then took my hand to his pink lips and kissed it "will you go out with me Gabriel?" , the way he said my name made the hair on the back of my neck stand up ,"yes eddy " , he hugged me tight warming up my cold skin.

***

Ed's p.o.v

" come on Dena , just a little" I extended my fangs out slightly ,"but-but you never drank straight from the vein ,I don't think you'll have the will power to stop" she pouted , "okay fine…you don't trust me" I retreated my fangs and turned around ,"don't be like that babe" she hugged me from behind and rubbed my torso "you know it's a sign of affection, and don't do that it's distracting" , "I know…it's just that the last time I let someone drink from me, they left me to die.." , I held her hands and turned around " sorry…I didn't know , but you know Sam and Jake are around and they can get me off you if I go all crazy maniac blood addict", she let out a deep breath "you're right…can I just go first?" , I smiled "absolutely honey" , I pulled her closer and tilted my head giving her a clear sight of my neck , she sniffed my hair a little then licked my neck , I flinched at her cold tongue against my warm neck "sorry" she whispered , I stroke her hair and felt her fangs extend out and she slowly dug them in my neck , it hurt at first but she quickly made it a pleasure and took away the pain , I relaxed and let her drink a little more before she pulled away and licked her reddish lips , "you taste so good" she said and I noticed the red and violet mix in her eyes slowly fading away as she took control again , I knew my eyes were their pure violet color I can't lie and say I didn't enjoy it , but now it was my turn "may i?" she nodded , I tilted her head on the side taking a good look at her delicious neck , I extended my fangs out then licked a spot on her neck , I could tell she was holding in a moan which made me grin , I bit her neck gently , she moaned and I made sure to not let her feel pain of my fangs piercing her skin ,she relaxed when I released a cold liquid in her vein to ease the pain , I took my time as I drank , making sure not to take too much to make her faint then I pulled my fangs out and licked the holes I made from her sweet blood , she held on to me when she felt my warm tongue against her cold skin "see? I told you I can handle it" I looked at her and smiled , "..hmm…yeah" , she opened her eyes and I smiled more at the view of her lustful violet eyes , she closed them then opened them again , they went from green to their normal grey color , and mine back to their usual black , she blushed " I've never done that before Ed" , "ohhh that's why you were so nervous" , "yeah" she blushed more , "I didn't hurt you did i?" I looked at her with concern , she smiled "no , you were perfect .

"I love you"

" I love you too"

A/N:Dena is Gabriel it's just her middle name :p

chapter twenty

✳ the bad girl's back*

Ed's p.o.v

I promised rose I'd help her practice her amazing new skill so here I was walking towards her room , "are you ready honey?" I yelled from outside the her door and suddenly the door swung opened with a crying rosy and puffed swollen red eyes " I miss mom..."she said between sobs , I hugged her tight and picked her up in my arms walking to her bed then sat down with her on my lap"shhht it's okay I'm here"she hiccupped a couple of time as I pated her back gently , she squeezed me tighter with her little arms around my neck "stop crying princess" I wiped her tears "i..i couldn't push it in the back of my head anymore daddy...I just had to remember her and deal with this..", "I know...you're mother loved you very much" she looked down "I remember when she'd come in my room when I had nightmares and we'd make a small tent with the sheets and eat march mellows until we fell asleep"I sad smiled sneaked into her lips" and when she made me tons of pancakes because I fell and cut my arm...she even made a bowl of ice cream to make me stop crying" I smiled " she was a great mom wasn't she?" , "you have no idea" she smiled.

Once in the practice field , I arranged some objects for rose to see how good her skill became with her little practices in her room ,so we made a fake fight preparation , I made a safe password if anyone gets hurt which is "strawberry" ...don't judge me I like strawberry , everyone was there, so the teams were :Sam , Jake ,Dena , Rosy and I against some guards but of course they wore protective suits because we were using real weapons .

Everyone took their position and got ready for the countdown "one...two..."I took a deep breath ,Dena stood in an attack position , rose concentrated and lifted some knives in the air towards the guards , Jake stood with his hands in his pockets like nothing's happening....little smug ,and finally Sam nodded for the Go signal "three!" I shouted and everyone yelled , ran , punched and kicked the enemy ,Rose sent knives towards the guards who played the dead once they got hit ,I laughed at that and almost had my royal ass kicked by someone, I jumped behind him "yoo hoo" I taped his sholder , he did the mistake of turning around which got him a punch from me , what? I don't play-fight in kill mode.

After practice we were all tired and sleepy , Sam was walking like a jelly fish , I walked and then stopped in the hallway, sat down and rested against the wall ,someone poked me" Ed wake up" , "umhh...dad I don't wanna go to school..the teacher smells like cow poop and dog food..." , I heard laughs and someone fell next to me , I opened my eyes and saw Sam rolling on the floor laughing "ehh...I hate school okay?", he laughed more "cow...poop....dog ...f-food" he said while laughing , I jumps on him with all my weight "who's laughing now daisy duck?".

After play-fighting my brother I needed to rest in fact everyone did , I just hope no one brakes in the castle because we'd just sleep it off and not wake up until someone pokes us or something so I took Dena to my room and went to sleep, sleep I said you pervs!

I rolled in bed trying to hide my face from the sunlight creeping from my bedroom window ,he's so adorable while sleeping, "well I'm awake now" I said while opening my eyes, she pouted ,I chuckled isn't she adorable? ,"stay out of my head" , "you know you look like a mad kitten right?" I smiled but it faded away when she slapped my chest hard , "ow, kitty's gat claws?" , I ruffled her hair and she speed pushed me with my wrists in her hands and smacked me against the wall ,"you bet she does" she grinned "you know I'm letting you hold me right? I'm much stronger" and it was true but I stood still "I'd like to see that" I grinned "your wished are my commands" and I speed pinned her on the bed with her wrists on the sides , I chuckled "now what are you going to do kitty?", she pouted and struggle but I held her tighter until she gave up and made and angry face, I let her go and she walked out of bed "oh come on! I was just playing around" , she ignored me , "really?" I speed hugged her from behind ,"I can't play-fight with my girlfriend?" I kissed her cheek , she tried not to smile but ended up giggle , "adorable "I kissed her shoulder "beautiful " I kissed her head "okay okay fine" I smiled but we were interrupted by loud bangs on the door "your majesty I'm very sorry to interrupt but we came back with the new born vampire you asked us to bring" a guard shouted from outside the door "she's here?" I shouted back ,"yes".

I pulled a shirt on while walking in the hallway with the guard on one side and Dena from the other , I turned in the corner towards the front door to see a tall girl with black long hair , white glowy eyes ,red little bit swollen lips , pale skin wearing a small top showing her belly and ripped jeans with black high heels, I froze"T-talia?"

chapter twenty one

✱ shocker come back*

Ed's p.o.v

"T-talia?"

I closed my eyes ,rubbed them hard and opened them again , "how can this be? You...you died!" , I walked closer to her , she raised an eyebrow "good to see you too"she said bitterly , "I'm-I'm.." , speechless I know...can you just tell your guards to let me go ? this is not the right way to treat a lady" , I closed my wide opened mouth before taking a deep breath "right...let her go she's not dangerous " , she chuckled at what I said , she laughed when I said she's not dangerous...so she thinks she is..wow where did the old talia go? , she dusted her arms like my guards were filthy , I grimaced at her then Dena came to stand next to me and whispered "is this...", "yes" , she stared at talia "I can hear you , you know" Talia said with a smirk on her face "b-but how is it possible ? I saw them kill you then ...then we couldn't find the body" , she sighed "I know Ed ...I know I'll try to explain to you as much as I remember ...look , at first it was total darkness then I heard a voice I couldn't concentrate on at first and everything in my body hurt...then he helped me...he took away the pain ..and –and I don't know...I just found myself like this"she looked at herself and gestured her hands around her body , I took my time to look at how different she looked...and acted , she wasn't the fragile and innocent girl I knew , she was a new person , a person I didn't know ,she noticed my glares " I know right? I look so different" she spun slowly "but I like it" she smiled wide " and I can do this" she raised her hand up and snapped her finger and a flame appeared on her palm "...you...i...eh do you know who he is? Or where he is?" , she put the flame out "no...he wore a mask and I didn't see him much, he found me when he needed to teach me things and left when he was done" she frowned "alright...umm Talia this is Dena...my girlfriend" , Talia looked socked at first but then she made a blank face and walked closer to us , Dena smiled at her "h-hi Talia right?" , Talia gave her hand to Dena and smiled "yes the dead wife" ,well...this is going good, not!.

Talia ,Dena and I walked through the hallways towards rosy's room , of course she's going to want to see her fourteen year old child , "oh my ..god" I heard a whisper behind us and quickly turned around to see a very shocked Sammy staring , "is that...really you?" he walked towards Talia looking up and down at her , before he could say anything else she was in his arms hugging him tightly "god Sam I missed your silly jokes" , he slowly wrapped his arms around her and smiled " and I missed your sassy attitude" , she let go of him and playfully punched his shoulder and he responded by poking her stomach , she giggled in a cute way then looked up at him " I'm going to see Rose...come with us?" it was more of a statement than a request so he simply nodded .

Don't freak out honey but...someone's here to see you , I mind spoke to Rosy on the way to her room while awkwardly holding Dena's hand, to be honest..i feel bad about this mess , if it's someone to see my skills I'm not opening the door dad, I let out a breath ,no...it's a family member...please don't have a heart attack ,after that there was no answer and I knew she shut me out of her head when I couldn't hear her thoughts.

Sam coughed awkwardly while we all stood staring at her door , no one making a the move to open the door or knock so he went for it , he made a melody knock that made me smile , it was the cue for each other to know it's her at his door or the other way around "come in uncle Sam" it felt weird that she called him uncle while she didn't look much younger than him, but what really annoyed me is that she said come in uncle Sam and not come in everyone while she knew we were all there , don't ask it's a vampire thing.

He opened the door and stuck his head in ,"hello my favorite niece" I could imagine her rolling her eyes at him "actually your only niece ", he chuckled then remembered why we were here and let the door open all the way , she jumped from her bed "who's that? she's pretty" she looked at Talia for a few seconds before looking at use confused on the reason we all stared at her "what?" , Sam elbowed me slightly "uhm...you didn't recognize her did you?...it's your m-" before I could continue Talia stepped in and stared right at Rose" hi Rosy" as soon as those words left her mouth Rose's eyes widened in shock , yeah I guess she recognized the voice " m-mom?".

A/N: alright I know I haven't updated in a looong time but I was very busy and wasn't in a writing mood so even if I forced myself to write it would have sucked...not like it's good anyways*sigh* sorry guys but anyways, I wanted to say vote and comment pretty please??? And tell me what you think about the pop twist and if you have ideas for the 23rd chapter cuz I have no idea...I hope you're enjoying my book so far oh and did you like the new cover? I made it myself but love_aixa a friend of mine pushed me to get a better cover so yea...okay I'll shut up now, bye.

Ps: the next chapter will be online in two days maximum , if my net doesn't go crazy.

Love , jenny-something

chapter twenty two

~ ~~~~~~

A/N:sorry I know I said two days but hey I have a life, so yeah here's the chapter don't forget to vote and comment or even message me if you want, enjoy!

Chapter twenty two :

dealing with the pain

Talia's p.o.v

I can't believe I'm back ,'wow', that's all I have to say ,Ed has a girlfriend not like it bothers me, I understand he's moving on slowly and I'm happy for him, of course a part of me still loves him but im not going to ruin his relationship now or ever.

Rosy's so grown up , god I missed her so bad , I'd look at the sky for hours thinking of her and wondering if she was doing the same , and wow lifting objects with her mind , that's my girl.

It's been three days since I came back ,everyone insisted that I stay at the castle ,this is going to be awkward , being around Ed and Dena, oh well..., I met Dena's baby brother , jake , he seemed nice , although he has a slightly big ego .

He didn't have to knock or say anything , I knew he was at my door so I just said "come in" while smiling at his saint , Sammy , "hey T " he popped his head in "hey Sammy, come in don't be a stranger" I smiled at him and he did the same closing the door gently behind him , "I wanted to ...see how you were doing" he looked down "I'm just fine don't worry about me , how are YOU?" I taped a spot next to me on the bed for him to sit on and he did so , he stayed silent playing with his fingers and looking down at them so I decided to break the silence "so anything new?" , he stopped his fingers and looked up with a sad face "yeah...this girl I accidently texted with a wrong number and talked on the phone a lot these few weeks and liked very much turned out to be a stupid werewolf who was trying to spy on us.." and he looked down again at his lap ,poor thing, "...I'm sorry" I wrapped him in a hug getting hugged back by him after a few seconds "its fine I just...I just wish someone would love me for me...not for the kingdom or this war..."

He put his head on my lap after braking the hug and stared up at me "you know ? you're the most kind and big hearted person I've known after my mother...I hope she comes back from that trip soon"he sighted , I rushed some hair stands off his eyes and forhead "do you miss her" , he stared into the distance"yeah...", "you're a great person Sammy you shouldn't care about a dog spy girl " , he chuckled " I know...but I really liked her T " , I smiled "so now we have nicknames for each other?" , he made a thinking face "hmm...maybe I should find something better then 'T' " .

I woke up to some music rubbing my sleepy eyes, I looked at the source of the music to see Sam smiling at me "sorry jake's calling me...so good morning sleepy head" , "it's morning?" my eyes widened "oh shit" , he chuckled "don't worry Dena told Rosy that you'll hang out with them when you wake up" , I frowned "I promised to kiss her good night" , he smiled a little "I know ...now excuse me I'll take this call and be back in a sec " , I got up lazily and noticed a leather black jacket falling from my shoulders , I picked it up and smiled at his saint .

chapter twenty three

Chapter twenty three:

Ed's p.o.v

the beginning of the end

"I can't believe she's here... "Dena said in a low voice , "me neither..." I replied looking at my lap "do you...do you still love her?" I looked at her "Gabriel i-" she cut me off "you know what? I don't want to know..." I sighted and looked down "it's not your fault you know" , I looked at her confused "what?" , "that she died...it's not your fault, it just happened "she smiled weakly , "I don't know what to think anymore honestly " I closed my eyes.

"dad I think we have company "I hear rosy mind speak to me, "what's wrong?" Dena asks "hmm?..."I look at her confused face "oh the humans are here for the meeting" , 'oh' was all she replied , I wore a nice black classic tuxedo while my dear lady wore a dark blue gallon , too fancy you say? Well I'm a prince and soon to be king so...nope!

We needed everyone on our side as the war is getting bigger and involving much more people than just the royal families , humans were on our side which is the main reason they're here today, to sign an arrangement , on the bad guys' side we have the stinking dogs and the ugly witches , what frightens me the most are having double agents around maybe even in the castle at this moment without me or anyone knowing on which side they were, that thought makes me nervous, my daughter's here , Gabriel's here , all my loved ones could be with the most dangerous person in the same room , "Ed.." , I float out of my thoughts " I'm fine" I took her hand in mine and start to walk towards the meeting room , nothing but the noise of her heels against the floor is heard down the hallways , echoed, calming to be honest ,although it reminds me of ticking clocks ,tick tock ,tick tock , alright now it's getting annoying , Dena lets go of my hand and I stop puzzled while looking at her , she smiles and lifts her leg behind her reaching her hand and taking off her beautiful black heels "I can tell it annoy you love " a smile creeps its way to my lips , she knows me so well ,"you know? You say you hate that I read your mind but you do the same in a similar way" , she takes off the other one and holds them with one hand while reaching to mine again ,I take her hand and bring it close to my lips kissing it gently lingering on her perfect skin, loving the way it feels on my lip before looking up at her, her beautiful loving eyes held such emotions , that amazing grey .

Everyone was there except for Rosy although she can hear everything from anywhere in the castle, she has sensitive hearing even to a vampire she's still young to have such powers, Jake kept glaring at the humans and it made the stinking smell of fear linger in the room , Sam was rather calm and...happy? , well who cares let's just settle this , Dena was calmly smiling at them , I think she was trying to assure them , a pretty lady is always reassuring although I wouldn't be if I was a hundred percent human in a room filled with blood suckers each with the strength of ten man, oh well, guess the lovely other girl who was there too? Yup Talia , I sighed silently just after glancing at her ,she looks nice...,anyways... my uncle was there too, well he IS the king after all, at least the human's king.

I signed after reading the entire thing but it didn't take long with my vampire eyes , and smiled while slowly giving the pen to one of the "important" humans who carefully took it with a fake smile , he signed as well"boo!" Jake half yelled lunching his body a little forward to the man who yelped like a little girl while he stepped away from the table , I glared at Jake with angry eyes "JAKE!" , he just shrugged and laughed , I stood up as I could see my uncle and Sam smiling and trying not to burst out laughing "I am very sorry, he's just a teen ager you know how they are" , I stepped closer to him very slowly while smiling apologetically , "please sit" I motioned towards his seat as he carefully walked by me , I glared once more at Jake who just smiled , "calm down Mark no one will hurt you here " my uncle spoke with a slight amusement in his tone I suppose to the human who turned into a scared kitten a few seconds ago, I sat down again while Dena leaned slowly to my ear "sorry..."she apologized for her baby brother , I smiled at her letting her know it wasn't a big deal.

After the meeting I insisted that we all have a meal together , I smiled as Dena warned Jake for the hundredth time if he does anything to scare our new allies , he chuckled I guess remembering what he did and she smacked the back of his head as he groaned , although I'm sure he didn't feel anything , it was the gesture that maters .

After eating we accompanied our guests to the gates and said our goodbyes ,everyone changed into more comfortable clothes and went to our rooms.

Talia's p.o.v

I changed into my night dress, silky white almost see through , I got this nice thing and some other clothes from Dena , I didn't like that idea trust me but it was all I could do for now, going shopping wasn't safe so...,I heard a knock on the door and smelled a familiar scent, I opened the door"hey...I wanted to check on you , you looked sad today...can I come in" , I opened the door more and move aside "im fine" , he closes the door behind him and looks at me with lust from head to toe "you look so...".

To be continued...

A/N:so who is it? Who's in her room at night while she's half naked ?

Vote and comment and did you like the long chapter or do you want the short ones? id love to hear yoour opinion.

love jenny_something

chapter twenty four

C hapter twenty four:

my savior

Talia's p.o.v

I coughed getting his attention back up to my face as I sat on my bed"you saw that im fine ...it's late" , he smirked and walks towards me and sits on the bed very close to me making our knees touch ,then he places his palm on my knee and starts trailing up my thigh making my silky dress move up with it and show most of my leg, I pushed his hand off and stood up "I think you should leave...now" he smirked wider and used his super speed to pin me to the wall with my wrists above my head "you have a very nice body" then he sniffs my hear in a disgusting way , I struggle but he was too strong, he kisses my neck slowly ,"stop!" it almost doesn't come out of my mouth , I hate this, feeling weak, I just hate it ,he put his hand under my dress and caresses my stomach "Jake stop it!" I yell, finally my voice came back , he smiles and ripped my dress with one move , I tried to knee him but he caught it ," bad girl you-"he didn't finish and the door swung open "let her go" I heard the muscular voice say , although I knew who it was I still wanted to see him but I couldn't with Mr. creep sanding tall covering my view so I tip toed and looked at towards the door frame and the silliest smile creped to my lips "Sammy.." I whispered ," this is none of your business Sam , go back to your room" Jake said not even glancing at him , he fixed his stare on my body , imagining all the sick things he'd do to me I assumed , I made a disgusted face, knew he was there was something fishy about him ,I told myself , Sam stepped forward with anger and red eyes consuming his face "I'll count to three....one" he said putting one finger in the air obviously struggling not to rip off Jake's throat , but Mr. creepy didn't move , "two..." I heard Sam steeping closer with a second finger up while Jake's hand traveled down my curves "three" Sam said impatiently after seeing the gesture Jake made, he clenched his fists and silence filled the room until Jake screamed with pain falling to the floor, I watched him as I put down my arms and rubbed my sore wrists , Jake kept screaming and rolling on the floor holding his stomach until he started coughing blood, dark black blood "..Sam" , Jake kept coughing and screaming "Sam!" he finally looked at me and the screaming stopped "are you okay?" he asked quickly , I nodded ,he looked back at Jake, "you have five seconds to leave this room and ten to leave the castle, if you ever come back I will personally rip your dead heart out...one" and Jake was out of sight , he sighted gazing at the floor "I'm sorry ... I just came back from a hunt , I'm sorry I didn't come earlier ..." he looked as if he done it with his own hands "it's okay you couldn't know he was such a creep.." I walked closer to him , he looked up and flushed when he realized I was in my underwear , oops ,he looked away shyly as I walked to my closet and tossed on a long shirt , I cleared my throat and he took the cue to look again "thank you Sammy " I smiled "you're welcome T " haven't found a nickname yet?" I grinned and pushed him with my shoulder playfully ,he smiled "no.." .

We talked for hours sitting on my bed ,legs crossed Indian style ,facing each other, this was nice, I could tell it was morning by the light coming from the window but I chose to ignore it and enjoy his company "...and then he threw me in the pool!" I threw my hands up in frustration by the memory of Ed and I , Sam burst out laughing ,rolling and holding his stomach "it was NOT funny" I whined with a childish voice , he laughed more "well you dared him to make you wet right there right then " he grinned , I blushed and looked down" I didn't mean it like that" , he chuckled but went serious right after "do you still love him?" he gazed at me, I was taken by surprised by that question , I thought about it for a moment ,do i? , I know I loved him before that's sure, he was my first love ...but do I still have feelings for him?, I looked up at him "no, I still care but I don't love him..." , I could see a smile forming on his face , his hand reached mine slowly and we intertwined our fingers , he made circles with his thumb on the back of my hand ,each one made me feel a tingle in my stomach and that's when I realized it...

I care about him.

I need him.

"What's on your mind?" his words pulled me out of my thoughts "hmm?" I wasn't back to reality just yet until he poked my cheek "you're thinking about something important...you play with your hair when you do that" he smiled , I do?, I noticed my free hand was twirling some of my hair , "oh..." I let go of my hair nervously not knowing what to do with my hand anymore," so...what is it?" he raised an eyebrow "what do you mean?" I answered , "what were you thinking of?" he pushed , I pressed my lips and looked around the room , his hand was very distracting at the moment , he loosened his grip but put his soft fingers back in the same position on my hand ,that earned another tingle that woke the butterflies in my stomach, I looked at him eyeing his handsome face , my gaze went to his arm that was showing from a sleeveless shirt , wow he has nice muscles, can I lick them? ,wait what?!,I blushed when I noticed I was staring , he chuckled , great! He noticed as well, perfect..., he came closer "you like my body?" he asked with a seductive low tone , I thought he couldn't get sexier? ,my eyes flew to his face wide opened , he grinned and put his lips close to my ear" 'cuz

I like yours" he said in the previous tone ,oh my gawd! ,I squealed/gasped in my head , I blushed even more if that was possible ,"i-" I started to say but he cut me "kiss me " he ordered , fine with me sexy thing…I need help , I cupped his cheek with my free hand and slowly came closer until our lips brushed gently , they started to move together excitedly , his tongue caressed my bottom lip asking for entrance which I quickly granted by opening my lips, he groaned when his tongue touched mine and caressed my cheek , suddenly we heard knocks on the door ,busted! , Ed stood there shocked and confused ,we jumped off each other , he raisend and eyebrow then cleared his throat "Sam…Talia".

chapter twenty five

Chapter twenty five:

I did not see that coming

Ed's p.o.v

Okay let me see if I got this right , my resurrected ex wife and my baby brother ,yeah that's about it...WHAT THE HELL?! , i hope I didn't say that out loud , my eyes kept going from Talia to Sammy ,well...this is interesting , I raised an eyebrow at them , expecting an explanation , why am I expecting one? It's not my business anyways ...okay stop staring and move along , they are free to do whatever they want , I finally convinced myself and spoke "alright...so we all heard what happened yesterday(vamp hearing) and Jake was kicked out , i wanted to throw him in the dungeon for a while but I respect Dena too much to do so sorry Talia , so...Dena wanted to talk to you and apologize " she nodded and I smiled a bit then left closing the door behind me , "that was awkward " I jumped from my spot to see my teen daughter grinning at me " I didn't know I could sneak on you dad" , I rubbed my face "god Rosy don't do that" she made and apologetic smile "sorry , anyways ...mom seems happy " she smiled happily "yeah...she looks like a teen in high school" I chuckled " I barely noticed that they had a thing going on" she sighed "so...want to race to the garden?"she grinned like a devil

"the old man still has skills you know? You really for it ?" I smiled "oh yeah I am" she made a salute to her forehead with two fingers out and stormed away towards the garden , I quickly followed "that's not fair!" she giggled "no one said it was a fair race " , I reached her but it was too late she already got there and was waiting for me leaning against the wall as if she waited for hours , "oh man" I whined , she chuckled "see? I am a good runner , all natural " she flipped her hair and batted her eyelashes "yeah yeah shut it you extremely talented daughter of mine " , she grimaced "I don't know if that was an offence or a compliment , we stayed silent for a bit and looked at each other then burst out laughing , she bent over and held her stomach tightly" you're ...such an alien sometimes " she said between laughs , I took a deep breath and whipped the tears from my eyes " , I put my arm around her shoulder smiling and walked her back into the castle "let's go princess"

.

Dena's p.o.v

Ed suggested to have a girls time with Talia and Rose which I was honestly nervous about, I mean come n I'm his girlfriend and she's his ex wife , I wonder if she still has feeling for him , oh well I wouldn't blame her if I was in her shoes , although I do feel threatened now she's back, she was his first love , I know how hard it is to forget and move on something so intense , but I trust Ed, its not like he's a big hungry wolf and she's a nice meaty sheep , I know him well if he still had feelings for her he'd tell , he would never lead me on ....right?

I knocked on Talia's door dusting my dress and heard her informing me to come in , I opened the door peaking my head in and smiled at her "hey" , she looked up from her desk and smiled at me "hey " I fully walked in and closed the door behind me "you ready? ", she bit her lip "oops I lost track of time …sorry I'll get ready real quick " , "it's cool I'll wait right here" I nodded and sat on her bed , she started super speeding everywhere and before I knew it she was in black leather pants and white loosed t-shirt that shower her left shoulder, red high heels that screamed "LOOK AT ME" ,some red lipstick on and dark eye shadow with eyeliner , her dark hair was loosed and pushed back , damn she looked like a model , does she always dress like this before going out or is it just me that she want someone's attention , oh well who cares? , "you look amazing " I looked at her wide eyed , she smiled "thank you , you look really good yourself " I smiled back , at least we were being nice just to look mature , "let's go have some fun" I hopped off the bed with a big grin .

Rosy was already waiting by the cars looking all bored , she wore a simple jean and black shirt with black sneakers , she had her long hair in a pony tail , damn I'm scared for her , it's just a day out but she's the princess , of course Ed sent like twenty build and muscular men with us , Sam insisted on coming along but laying low to let us have "girls time" ,there was six cars including ours , we had some security guard with us and Sam who was driving , the three of us were in the back quietly chatting on random things , poor Rose was being home schooled so she didn't really have any friends ,but believe me she wasn't the shy silent girl you'd think she was , I learned some knew things about Talia , that she was a maid in Ed's castle which was the humans' before he found out he wasn't all human , the thought of her with him alone made me angry and jealous , but that's in the past I shouldn't hold it against her.

I lifted up my gaze from Rosy who was telling her mother about a memory she had with her dad , I noticed Sam taking glances from time to time at Talia , there was something going on that I didn't know , and to be honest I was so curious to find out I almost squealed , yes me squealing…weird I know .

A/N:ouuuu girls day out next chapter , excited? Cuz I am! , shout out to girls day out? , anyways there will be some thrilling things coming up watch out *wiggles eyebrows*, some romance between the new couple ish ? of course! I'm a sucker for cheesy romance sue me :p

Love you all , *throws candy and pop corn at you*

- -

C hapter twenty six:

*to spy or not to spy *

Unknown's p.o.v

I watched as the girl or should I say woman who would soon be mine and under my control laughed , she walked around the mall ,they closed it for other people because of the princess , rich little brat .

At least my girl was obviously having fun , I watched her smiles giggle and laugh , it was so damn hard to not just jump out of my hiding place and hold her, once I get her under my commands and finally take what's mine : the throne , I will be the king and she will be my queen .

Soon my dear , soon we will rule together , all you have to do is be my double agent and tell me every small thing that happens inside that castle , soon Ed will be out of my way , and so will Sam.

Rose's p.o.v

This is nice, being out with mom and Dena , oh mom I missed her so much , I still can't believe she's here , I'm just scared I'll wake up tomorrow and this would be just a dream , dad wasn't here thought ,I'd love it if he was but he always has work and meetings or he's spending time with Dena , not that I hate her or anything , I really like her , and he does spend time with me , a lot but who'd have enough of a dad like mine? , not me anyways, maybe that's why everyone loves him and wants to be with him , that makes me think of him and mom , I looked at the outside of a store , a beautiful red dress sat on the manikin , why didn't they get back together? , he really loved Dena didn't he? , my floating questions were interrupted when I walked in something hard , warm , it moved , hmm?, his hands held my waist so I don't fall , and I can't say that bumping into him was all that got me off balance , because when I put my hands on his chest to lift my head and look at him , I swear I almost fainted , blue sky eyes , dark black hair , full pink lips... wait a minute! , why am I looking at his lips? , okay I should look away now , at least push myself off him , no? ,hehe my body just said no..., "are you okay?" his deep voice pulled me out of my daydreaming and misunderstanding between my brain and body "hmm?....oh yeah I'm good thanks for catching me " , he smiled and let go of me "you're welcome princess but please forgive me for touching you without permission ", he stepped back and put one hand on his stomach and stretched the other one on his side then bowed "my name is j-" he was cut off by my dear mother who called and almost yelled from the side of the mall "Rosy we're leaving , there's plenty more of that around town " I flushed red , mooom , he stood up ,his large shoulders stiff, I screamed internally ,why now? Isn't it enough I never go out or go to a school like everyone else and don't meet people or boys that I didn't even get his name or number, I groaned inside my head as I paced up to my mom and Dena , I looked back at the gorgeous guy frowning slightly but it was quickly replaced by a smile when I waved at him , he waved back ,aww man can I have him for my birthday ? ,I liked him sue me ,plus you'd say the same if you were in my place believe me .

Talia's p.o.v

I kept gazing at Sam the entire day , he looked so good worrying about us and looking everywhere his dark reddish hair falling on his eyes , his black eyes scanning the mall smoothly ,his arm muscles flexing every time he brushes his hair or takes a shopping bag for us , yeah he was the time to carry a bag for a lady , I glanced at his neck which moved slightly with his pureblood pulse , I felt my mouth go dry and my fangs threatening to come out ,I wanted his blood and I wanted it now , I heard before that a pureblood's blood is the sweetest you could find , I wonder if he wants mine too.

I walked quickly heading outside to get fresh air and maybe find away to control my urge ,"mom slow down you're almost running" I heard Rose whine behind me, "she's right Talia slow down" Dena added , but I needed to get away from there , from him .

A/N: who's the name of the boy Rose met? Will they meet again or never? What race is he? Will Talia control herself or end up in a blood bath? Who's the "unknown person ?will the mall open tomorrow? Lol just kidding , leave your answers and expectations please.

Love you all *throws clothes and handsome boys at you*

chapter twenty seven

C hapter twenty seven:

*my secret urge *

Taia's p.o.v

I could see the door, I was almost there until...until Sam blocked my way , I gasped at the his sudden appearance , I looked back "what the...? , weren't you there just now?" I turned to him again to see his annoyed face "we're vampires remember? " all I could say was 'oh' , well I'm so smart, not! ,"why are you running from me?" oh crap , I totally forgot I was trying to be far from him but now I'm closer than ever" i-I ....i" I could feel my fangs starting to slide out but I quickly covered my mouth hiding them from Sam , my gum felt like it was being stabbed with needles over and over again , I jogged to Gabriel "where's the bathroom?" I asked quickly still covering my mouth with my palm , she pointed at the left to a small hallway , I ran through to finally come to a night sky blue door, I jerked it open , I looked at myself in the mirror , my pupils were dilated ,red and black mixing through them , you could see the veins around my eyes and under them , my fangs were sharp and white , I inhaled a big breath although I don't need one nor does my heart beat ,I clenched the sink tightly then opened the tab and splashed some water on my face , I heard the door open and close , I looked in the mirror to see a sad Sammy "what did I do?" he asked with a hushed voice , aww poor thing though he looks cute sad ,by this time I was almost fully normal "i...it's not...we.." he hugged me tightly from behind and buried his handsome face in my hair taking a sniff , not weird at all , placed my hands on his which were resting on my stomach and closed my eyes "Sammy...it's not you , it's me , I...", It was so embarrassing to tell him that I was craving his blood , it might seem weird to humans but hey I was one not long ago but I guess I'm starting to understand these vampire things better , I heard it was what couples do to show their affection to one another , does that mean my subconscious wants to show him that I care? ,I do care but that's a strange way to show it , plus it felt more of a need to taste his blood, wondering how it would taste , sweet? Salty? Metallic? , I guess that there was one way to find out right?

I opened my eyes and slowly started to speak as he was silent all this time letting me find the right words to say what I needed to say "I'm craving your blood " I watched his head rise slowly from my hair to look at me in the mirror , his face held a surprised look that vanished in a few seconds after my words sunk in and it was replaced with a smile , he leaned down and brushed my hair off my neck and kissed it gently letting his lips linger there before pulling away and turning me to face him ,he observed my face for a moment before he finally spoke "I want you too" and with that he kissed me the most soft and gentle kiss I ever had , he held me so carefully as if I was made of bubbles and could explode at any minute , the kiss became deeper and more urgent as our tongues brushed against each other he slowly pushed me to the wall until I felt his strong arms on my thighs and he picked me up easily like I was made of cotton candy , I quickly wrapped my arms around his neck and my legs around his waist afraid I would fall , he chuckled at my worried face "trust me" he murmured against my ear and I melted at his deep husky voice then I felt my back rest on the cold bathroom wall ,he tilted his head to the side giving me a nice view of his neck as he traced his hand on his soft skin he said "go ahead ".

I could feel my gum hurting again , my fangs slowly sliding out without any warning , I could see his veins better , I could hear his blood racing through his neck and I wanted to taste it, you know what's the best part of it? Now I could .

I sunk my fangs into his neck , which got me a wince from Sam , oops I guess that was too deep , I instantly closed my eyes when the metallic liquid made contact with my tongue , oh how sweet he tasted , I couldn't get enough , I kept sucking on his wound wanting for more , and I knew my eyes were a mix of red and lusty violet , I heard him moan but that wasn't good, because it made me even more excited ,he was getting weaker , he had trouble holding me up , suddenly it didn't seem like such a good idea ,"T-talia" I heard him call , and I knew it was my warning that I had taken too much , I forcefully pulled back resting my head on the wall behind me my eyes still closed , I licked my bloody lips , delicious , I was breathing heavily and so was he .

He placed me down gently as I opened my eyes to look at him ,his eyes were pure purple , I see I'm not the only one who got excited , I smirked and pulled my fangs in "you taste so good" I couldn't help myself from stressing the 'good' in a $exy female tone that made him bite his lip "I think it's my turn t-" he was cut off by knocks on the door" you guys okay?you've been gone for more then fifteen minutes "Dena half shouted from outside , I felt like a teen caught doing naughty things with a boy at school , wow.

A/N: so *wiggles eyebrows* how did I do? , shout out to drinking blood? No? it's creepy? Okay *sad face* anyways schools starting soon oops I mean hell *smiles* which means there wont be much updates of blood prince *lays down and cries* but I will try to write whenever I'm free and don't have my mom on my heels *looks around paranoid * aaaaand Blood prince will be coming to an end soon , like four more chapters and viola , you guys want a sequel or nah? If you do please let me know , and if I do write a sequel it would be about a future couple *zips my lips* nope , love you all bye!

throws kisses and heavy make outs at you(because throwing blood would be too much for you guys to handle)

chapter twenty eight

✻ my boss?!

Sam's p.o.v:

We walked holding hands towards the big wooden door and waited for the guards to open them as she looked at me smiling I winked and she giggled , dear god she giggled I've never heard her giggle before "I've never heard you giggle T " she titled her head to the side "really?" I answered "yeah" I smiled and she did too , I realized we've all been standing there for too long...something was wrong , I knocked on the door and waited , nothing , I knocked again harder but no one opened "something's wrong...", talia squeezed my hand "what should we do ?"she asked , I pushed her gently behind me a little further "we go in and watch out for Rosy "I kicked the wooden doors flying wrecked ahead of us , Talia and Dena put Rose in the middle of the two of them and got ready for some steamy fighting , I pulled out my silver daggers and walked in "I bet someone let the dogs out"I grinned , gosh I hate those self absorbed stinky puppies , I sniffled the air "werewolf"I warned the girls ,my ear twitched when i heard some growling and low howling further ahead , I turned my head towards everyone and motioned them to be silent with my index finger pressed against my lips ,

Talia and Dena both nodded so I got ready for the fight and walked ahead , I knew we vampires don't really have a smell but on the other hand Rose being a highbred has a smell of her own which means we will be detected even if we don't make any noise , "I'm sorry…"I heard Rose say sadly , I turned to her confused "wh-" , "I make everything hard for you guys , you always try to protect me and I screw it up just by being me.." , I realized she had been reading my thought "I don't protect you because I have to , I protect you because I love you and if I ever have a child I know Ed would die to protect him/her , that's how family goes Rosy , plus I think you're way stronger than me anyways you should be the one protecting us " I assured her knowing how depressed she felt , she looked up shyly "yeah…you're right"and poof she was gone before I could flex a muscle "Rose! " Dena cried out , I super sped after her hearing whimpers and loud screams , if I had a heart it would have exploded , I rushed in the kitchen to find Rose standing with her back to me while breathing heavily then I noticed a limb body laying in front of her and at the corner of my eye I could see a young werewolf boy hissing at us but too scared to attack , I felt Talia and Dena by my side and with one swift move they killed the wolf splashing his blood on the yellow painted wall , "Rosy ?" I walked closer around her and looked at her bloodied hands and mouth , her fangs were extended out and dripping with blood , she wiped her mouth with the back of her hand then opened the tab and washed her hands and face then headed out to her room on my guessing , I noticed Ed walking in sweaty and bloody "hmm…I don't think she needs bodyguards anymore"I said .

Talia's p.o.v:

We were just done with cleaning up the mess that happened after the fight , I flexed and yawned "god I'm tired ,sleepy and hungry " everyone nodded agreeing with me then Rosy flashed in my face making me flinch "lord…you need to stop being so creepy hun you'll give me a 'heart attack' " I giggled at my joke knowing my heart is dead already but Rose looked irritated "mom...listen to me , I hear someone else's thoughts , I mean someone other than all of you or the maids or the guards ... a vampire to be specific " , I looked at her amazed and also worried and confused of how we could have not sensed him , "the dining room " she said and disappeared as we all followed right away.

Appearing in the dining room we found no one , we kept looking around until we heard someone clapping and laughing hysterically, I froze "no...it can't be" , thud after thud his footsteps came closer behind me "you look wonderful Talia ...so good looking" I turned around to see a tall strong man eying me up and down "how did you know I live here?" I asked backing away slightly , I walked into a solid chest , his arms wrapped around me protectively and he whispered in my ear" I'm here" his voice immediately relaxed me but I was quickly back to reality when victor answered my question while narrowing his eyes at my Sam "is that a way to welcome your maker?...and i followed you babe" I felt Sam's fangs extend near my ear and heard his warning hiss "don't call her babe " he looked at Sam dead in the eye and laughed loudly as if he told him the funniest joke on the planet "what do you want?!" I shouted over his laughter , he stopped and looked at me "you ." he said like it was the most obvious thing ever , I felt Sam's arms tighten around me trying desperately to show his claiming , victor flashed in my face and kissed my lips before I could move a muscle then he stood back in his place , nope, you ain't getting away with that so easily ,I extended my claws and fangs and slipped down from Sam's grip heading towards the bastard as fast as I could , he only smiled which made me even angrier , I directed my claws at his face wanting to tear it apart but all I could do was leave a tiny scratch before he disappeared .

Back to my room after victor left I watched Sam from the window as he punched and kicked everything on the training field, he broke and shred everything and it didn't take a genius to know he was pissed so I let him cool down, I sat on my bed and heard a weird paper noise so I got up to find that I sat on an envelope, I took it and laid down while opening it, I pulled out the letter that was inside .

Dear babe,

I've missed you so much since you ran away leaving me alone after I made you an undead and taught you all you know now from how to fight to how control your anger , I see you still have an issue concerning the matter , but I needed to tell you that you're acting was so well that even I thought you really cared about them , the royal trash .

We can have our own empire after you help me take theirs down , you'll be my eyes and ears from the inside won't you beautiful? ,I shall leave you to your spying and angry lover I presume , enrevoire ma belle Talia.

Ps: your lips taste wonderful .

Love V

chapter twenty nine

---

* who are you really?*

Ed's p.o.v:

I sat down next to Gabriel wrapping my arms around her and watched Rosy doing her daily practice of throwing knifes and daggers, and of course she was using mostly her powers, I wonder who that guy was and how Talia knows him...maybe Ed knows what it's all about , would he tell me though?, I looked at Gabriel "of course I would" I answered her thoughts , she looked at me for a moment then went back to watching Rose , for a second it seemed as if she blocked me out of her head, but then again she could do that if she concentrated hard enough , but I started hearing her thoughts again but they were blurry and selected , as in things she only allowed me to hear so I decided to stop listening and got up .

I knocked on Talia's door and waited ,I heard some noise then footsteps coming closer, the door swung open ,I looked at a very nervous Talia as she grabbed my arm and pulled me inside in a hurry then checked the hallway and dismissed the guards who were standing near, she closed the door and turned towards me then sighed "I need to tell you something" .

"um…when I was killed ,the werewolves threw my body near a river …and the vampire guy..victor, found me and turned me , he kept me under control most of the time , he taught me how to control my thirst , how to fight ,how to use my fangs and claws …basically everything I know about being a blood sucker" she smiled slightly ,I pressed her hand "I know it was hard for you and I'm sorry…I'm so sorry Talia ,It was my job to protect you and it still is but I failed " she shook her head quickly "don't you ever say that again Ed"I smiled , "so why did you run away from him?" she looked down and frowned "he…he made me hunt humans ,we would wait in a dark alley or a forest road at night and attack people ,we'd keep them awake and suck their blood until there was no more..but that's not what I need to talk to you about" I looked at her waiting for her to get there , "well…this evening when I got back to my room I found this " and she handed me an envelope .

After reading that bastard's letter I told her I would think of a way to handle this and doubled security near her room and told her it would be better is Sam stayed with her , she bit her lip nervously "okay " she said shyly .

I went back down outside to Rose and watched her for a moment before saying "you should work more on your close distance abilities Rose" I walked closer , she turned and smiled "and the old man is going to teach me?"she said sarcastically "ouch…"I shook my head and smiled "ready?" I questioned " uh huh " she answered and with that we got into a fierce fight , of course I didn't hurt her I just showed her how fast her enemy can be and that she couldn't just use her long distance fight techniques .

Once done I went in my bedroom ,and in the bathroom i turned the cold water on then I took off my shirt letting it fall on the floor , I took off the rest and stepped under the shower letting the water work its way down my body , I knew she was behind me , watching but I didn't want to turn to her, she finally made up her mind and joined me wrapping her delicate

hands on my abs ,she rested her head on my back , "I love you " she said ,
"I love you too".

chapter thirty

---

 the final battle* PART ONE

Ed's p.o.v

I smiled at the sudden change in her mood , Dena doesn't usually act like this , but at least she's in a good mood now .

After having some fun and showering I put on clean clothes and watched her getting dressed , pulling up her silky night gown , all the way up her long pale legs , I couldn't help but stare , she smiled sweetly at me "you know...I can't wait to have little things running around the castle.." she simply said while slipping in bed ,oh I totally forgot about the corona-tion...which means I need a queen ...oh god here we go again .

I couldn't sleep that night , I just stood on the balcony thinking while taking in the view of the forest and the moon's reflection in the lake , suddenly I saw some branches move near the gates , then I saw a shape walking away , a woman , Talia .

*after 30 minutes * Sam's P.O.V

I had to admit..i was jealous , how could that jerk talk to MY Talia like that? , I wasn't going to stand there and watch him steeling her into the enemy side..and his side , so I decided take my brother's advice when he told me to spent the night with her with the excuse of "you have a blood sucker and the whole werewolf empire after you and us" .

I took a few breaths trying to calm down while I stood at her door ready to knock when the door swung open showing a very frustrated Talia , "won't you f***ing get in already?! You've been standing here for five minutes , with your loud beating heart and heavy breathing " ,I was taken by surprise and stepped back being straddled by her sudden frustration "i-i-I was thinking..." I tried to justify myself feeling like a kid that's done something wrong .

She sighed and stepped away letting me through " come in." , I walked in her room silently sitting on the bed and watched her swiftly hide a paper in her desk , wow she forgot I'm a vampire and can see her in super speed? , I didn't question it and decided to let it be .

After a while of talking and laughing (and heavy make out sessions) we thought it would be best to go to sleep , I was too nervous to stay so I got up , "alright...goodnight " she grabbed my wrist tightly "s-stay.." and that was all it took me to not lose her out of sight for the next ten hours or so .

I laid there cuddling her in my arms , my cold skin touching hers , she let out a soft sigh as if she was relieved by having me so close , I closed my eyes and kissed her cheek before drifting off to a deep comfy sleep.

I woke up to an empty bed , "T? where are you? " I rubbed my sleepy eyes and sat up looking around the room and searching for her scent or energy , nothing "I wonder where she went...".

Once showered and dressed I drank some blood and started looking for Talia , I walked in the sorta-hug-living room to find Gabriel weeping and saying "yes. Of course I would " , " Dena? Ed? What's going on? " they looked at each other as she wiped her tears then both looked at me and said in synch "nothing."

After a few minutes of reading and talking with Ed and Dena a messenger arrived "your majesty ...it began " , Ed clenched his fists and stood up "alright then...we are ready" he replied , we went in the weapons room and armed ourselves to the neck , everyone was fighting , even Rose , although Ed didn't want her to , she just said she'd break out and he knows it so he agreed .

It was twelve and a half when we left the castle , still no sign of T , I was worried sick , I just hoped she wasn't...no don't even think about it , we could see them now, the werewolf army was a few miles ahead as we kept moving forward , the humans were on our side , thank god the king is Ed's uncle , I know humans aren't powerful, they have no powers, no sensitive hearing , no super sight or speed , but with all those humans , they can make a difference.

chapter thirty

C hapter thirty:

*the final battle*PART TWO

Sam's P.O.V

We lunched forward , vampires super speeding and humans using normal speed , some carrying rifles and machine guns and others holding daggers and arches , the two sides of the battle collided , blood splashed around , screaming echoed through the wind , my heart ached every time I had to slice someone's neck open , they whimpered and growled and howled , but I didn't stop , how could I knowing that some of them took away Talia's chance to be human, to grow old with her kid and Ed , suddenly I felt a wave of anger coming out of my dead heart , sadness , sorrow and pain , they killed her , they killed my love , yes now I am sure , I love her .

I killed hundreds and they were still coming, I was starting to lose hope , I stood still for a while , covered in blood , my hands dripping with blood , "where are you?" I mumbled under my breath , I heard someone yelling , but I couldn't move anymore I was tired and depressed , it seemed like we weren't going to see the sunrise today ,maybe it's better like this...she might be dead already who knows? I better give up now before it's too late.., I opened my eyes and looked up to see Ed shouting at me " Sam! Look at me! Snap out of it for god's sake!" he shook me back and forth , I opened my mouth to reply but then I noticed something behind him...I couldn't believe my eyes , it can't be happening , not now ,how could she do this to me? I thought she was on our side.

There stood Talia with that Victor guy with his arm around her , some werewolves and some vampires stood beside them , oh so I'm the idiot ,I thought , Ed noticed my gaze as he turned to look behind him and stared at the smirking bastard "Talia." He greeted calmly "Ed." She replied not moving from her place , "where were you?" I spoke walking closer ignoring the hisses from the werewolves and vampires on the bad guy's side , she looked away and stayed silent " what? You can't even say it in my face? That you used me like a toy? That you never really stopped working for him?!" I was shouting now , I couldn't hold back anymore , tears were leaking out of my eyes , and I didn't really care how broken I looked , I wanted her to see it , to see how she crushed me.

Then she looked up but not at me, behind me and nodded slightly, what the..?, as I looked behind me Ed lunched past me and at the werewolves shredding them , Rosy took two vamps and Dena three other , I looked back to Talia to see her pulling her hand out of victor's chest "I told you you won't get away with that kiss, my lips only belong to him" she whispered softly in his ear then released his heart on the floor and faced me once again.

Ed patted my shoulder but I was still confused and kept looking from one to another "what just happened? " everyone smiled then Dena came closer and rubbed my back gently " it was a trap , she was a spy for them yes but she told them false information and told what they were really up to"she told me.

I frowned and looked at Talia with teary eyes " and you all couldn't have told me ?!" she flinched slightly at my anger , Ed gripped my arm tightly " we had to not let you find out or you would have ruin the plan..I'm sorry brother I'm the only one to blame".

I calmed down and whipped my face and eyes then turned around ready to leave but someone bumped into my back hard and wrapped two arms around my waist and she cried furiously , like a little kid , "i-I'm sorry... please don't do this to me I c-can't I can't live without you" she confessed.

I sighed softly "I love you silly " I said as I turned to face her and pulled her closer and held her tight " I l-l-love you too " she said sniffling , "let's go home" I told her , she nodded .

chapter thirty one

✳ back to safety*

Talia's P.O.V

The day after the battle squeezed my heart with pain , when I saw all those dead bodies laying on the ground, werewolves , humans and vampires , we all sacrificed a piece of our souls to have a taste of peace and safety again , mothers cried for their sons , wives cried for their husbands and children cried for their fathers , my heart ached just from the thought .

Someone waved a hand in my face bringing me back to reality "Talia ? hello?" Gabriel spoke , "oh ..sorry I was lost in thought , what were you saying?" I smiled apologetically , "I said are you coming with us to the village tonight?" , after the battle we tried getting things back in order and fixed people's houses , Ed ordered to distribute a share of money to everyone who's had their homes damaged or destroyed or lost a family member .

So tonight as we were finally done with everything we would have a ball near the village " of course " I answered anxious for the event , Gabriel giggled and nudged me in the side "Romeo is staring at you again" she nodded her chin towards Sammy who was totally in another world , "hey Sam think fast!" she shouted at him and threw an apple at him which she just picked up from a bowl on the table near us , he was too slow to wake up from his daydreaming and received a full hit in the face and tripped backwards landing on his back "owww" he groaned , I sped to him and put his head on my lap "are you okay? " he grinned " now I am " .

Ed's P.O.V

Sam and I stood by the stairs in the ball room waiting for Gabriel and Talia to go down , everyone was here , humans , vampires and even some werewolves who actually stood by us in the fight , they wanted peace and knew their kind was ruining it for everyone .

Someone elbowed me on the side gently ,I turned to look and saw Sam looking forward and smiling wide, I turned my attention to what got him so happy , Gabriel walked down wearing a tight long red dress that made her curves show , it was lacy on the top part in black and silky on the down part in red , next to her was Talia with a black front opened dress that had its straps hanging on the sides of her upper arms , the lacy part was on her belly , showing a little of skin since it was almost see through , now I see why Sam is smiling so wide, we had the most beautiful women as dates tonight .

I gave my arm to Gabby who happily took it carefully holding it as we walked gracefully towards the VIP section and next was Talia who took Sammy's arm and decided to dance before sitting , I saw them happily talking as everyone stared at the couple slow dancing.

Talia's P.O.V

I could barely focus as I felt his gentle hands holding me as we danced , "you look so beautiful" I flushed at his words "you don't look so bad yourself " I giggled looking a his fine body in a tuxedo , he looked gorgeous with a white shirt and a black jacket , pants , fancy shoes and a tie , a silky red handkerchief , he noticed my gaze and chuckled "you like the fancy clothes? oh yeah about that , I noticed Ed and Dena had matching colors but you don't have red anywhere "I giggled and whispered in his ear "just because you can't see it it doesn't mean I'm not wearing red" he was surprised by that and made a funny noise, I giggled "my little devil , you've learnt to stop being shy" he replied .

After the dance we sat down in the VIP area with Ed, Dena , uncle Charlie and his wife , every now and then someone approached us to thank us for all of what we've done through the battle , it was nice to finally see all the races agree and live in peace , I noticed Rose was in a corner talking to a boy and blushing madly , oh well she had to grow up sometime but what I couldn't help but notice was Dena wearing a new ring.

chapter thirty two

C hapter thirty two:

*the coronation *

Dena's P.O.V

I rubbed my sleepy eyes and sat up in bed , this was going to be a long day , lord help me , Ed groaned next to me after I started tickling him "noooo I don't want to get up , let me sleep" I pouted and glared at him , fine. I thought aware that he could hear it and got up stumbling my feet loudly and making as much noise as I could , it was early indeed , but hey we're getting married we need to get ready.

After a few thuds and booms Ed finally got up , showered and put on some clothes ,he ate some food and had the barber over for a haircut , Sam joined him because he was the best man of course and I got together with Talia and Rose , doing our hair , makeup and picking the right dresses for them as well , my dress was a yellowish princess dress with a pearl necklace and shiny diamond decorated high heels , I checked the fancy dresses we had to chose from to Talia and Rosy , "hmm...too long....too short...too dark.." and it went on and on from dress to dress until I saw two dark blue dresses

, knee length ,slightly opened in the front ,held up by straps "perfect" I moved my hand along the silky fabric as " Rose and Talia squealed "we love them! " Rosy exclaimed as Talia said" you have a great taste Gabriel I'm glad it didn't go like in movies where the maids of honor end up with ugly dresses.

Ed's P.O.V

After the whole wedding ceremony we went through the coronation of me becoming king and my dear wife becoming the queen , my step mother windy witnessed everything in silence casting a smile every few minutes and wishing us the best at the end of the day .

I couldn't believe I was married again , the wedding went great , and the coronation as well , I loved it when Gabby put a little joke in there to crack up all the emotional feelings that were forming in the room , finally our lives are perfect again .

*****Walking up to the balcony as I hit the answer button I can't help but smile hearing my annoying brothers voice "so how does it feel to be a married man?" He asked " Not So Different I'd say" I said turning back to look at my Sleeping beauty buried between the Sheets

"How are things there?" I rubbed my head wondering if we had any trouble at the horizon " stop worrying I told you I've got this especially that we..." I blocked his voice out when I saw her waking up " right listen I have to go take care.."

****

Epilogue

*two years later *

Ed's P.O.V

"honey come quick ! he's walking on his own!" I appeared in the living room with my dear wife and watched Jaden take slow clumsy steps towards mommy ,"yay my little man did it !" I exclaimed and picked him up throwing him in the air and winced as I heard Gabriel screaming at me "oh my god be careful ! he's so little you can't just hold him like that , you could have-" and she was interrupted by a knock on the door , I watched the couple walking in , a shy Talia and a grinning Sammy .

We sat down , Gabby holding Jaden on her lap and Sammy and Talia holding hands quietly , "so.." I began "what's going on with you two?, you're being too silent today " I said looking from one to the other , I watched as Talia mumbled under her breath to Sammy shyly "you tell them" He nodded smiling and faced us still holding her hand tightly "we're getting married!" he said jumping from his seat , I got up and hugged him happy that he found someone to spend his life with "congratulations Sam , I'm so happy for you two" I said ," oh man you have no idea how nervous I was to ask 'the' question " he replied glancing at her .

The End.